by Be

CHAPTER 1

Danny Rawlings refused to believe he was dead.

The body was sat hunched over the wooden desk, forearms and brow pressed flat to the surface now awash with a glistening slick of blood trickling over the edges to patter on the hardwood floor below – as if the old man had raised his arms to surrender only for his pleas to go ignored. The lounge curtains were still drawn.

The thought that he was responsible suddenly made him heave.

He couldn't stop the knife in his hand from shaking. His grip tightened round the handle as his eyes returned to the blood up the white wall behind the desk. The messy strokes and smears of red were like a child's finger painting yet he could read it well enough:

XII

A parting message to the world, Danny reckoned.

What was he trying to say?

A plain calendar, correctly open on January, was hanging above the morbid graffiti. One of the days had been circled.

Danny leant as close as he could without leaving a footprint in the blood. It was the fourteenth. *Today's date!*

The box beneath had been left blank. Who had he planned to meet or what had he planned to do?

Danny guessed it wasn't to die.

What have I done?!

Danny's eyes darted back down to the desk. He made sure not to get too close, aware the body might keel sideways onto him.

Through the eerie gloom, he could see a shut laptop with the sticker *PROPERTY OF THE BRITISH HORSERACING AUTHORITY* on its silver lid.

Nearby he could make out a plastic lanyard and the stub of a racecourse ticket. Also bathed in blood was the handset of a phone lying halfway between its dock and the victim's head.

3

He listened for the small purr of a dial tone but it was a female voice eerily repeating over and over, 'Please replace the handset and try again'.

Neatly lined up against the wall at the back of the desk was a row of weighty formbooks full of horseracing results and statistics, blood yet to spread that far. Alongside the books, there was a pile of colourful metal badges or medals that had cascaded from a glass jar on its side.

The man's lifeless face was a like a still photo, gone was the strained look of anguish that had slowly eaten away at him. He really was now resting in peace.

And Danny knew the answers he craved had also died here.

His thumping heart felt like it was trying to escape his ribcage and his face was tingling with sweat, as if he'd just run a marathon. Panic had set in.

Although a convicted housebreaker in his youth, nothing could have prepared him for this.

Yet part of him still couldn't tell for sure if this was actually happening. Perhaps he had fallen asleep watching a late-night horror movie. He hoped someone would wake him up or at least change the channel.

He simply couldn't bear being away from wife Meg and miss seeing Jack and Cerys grow up, pass exams he never got the chance to do, even go to college or get married.

How the hell would they cope with me inside? Get a grip, man! No time for weakness. Think!

Suddenly he felt a survival instinct kick in. No way was he going to be sent down for this.

He noticed the man's fingers were bent and spread like a spider, as if he was trying to scratch the table, cracked fingernails embedded in the veneer of the wood. Was he trying to scratch the murderer's name? Or was he just deflecting some of the pain away from his other injuries?

It's only then Danny saw something small and shiny under there. He used his smartphone to shine some light. As he looked closer, it appeared to be a shiny medal of gold and enamel. He couldn't pick it up without moving the hand. The fingers were acting like the bars of a cage. The man's broken nails in the wood suggested he wanted this protecting above all else, including himself.

Danny tilted the phone slightly. Between the bloody fingers he could now make out it was a maroon badge, square, with the corners clipped. There was black writing embossed on it in gold: *Middlesex County Racing Club*. The words were displayed in an arc across the top, above the year 1966 and the number 34.

That was the year England won the World Cup, Danny thought. He had little else.

The badge's centrepiece was a black shield, an emblem or coat of arms. Set against the black were three gold-hilted curved swords, each with a notched single blade, like a scimitar. Danny recognised the coat of arms from Middlesex Cricket Club.

At the top of the badge, a black and red striped string cord had been threaded through a gold loop, presumably to hang it from the lapel buttonhole in a suit.

Was it valuable? Perhaps, he thought, but valuable enough to protect with your life?

Danny looked over at the other badges that had spilt from the cranberry bowl by the formbooks. Why pick out that one above all others?

He dry swallowed. He could control the nerves circling down at the start of a big race, but there was more at stake now.

Suddenly, a distant rattle of glass came from the back of the house.

Shit!

The kitchen door, Danny reckoned. He'd just come from there. He could no longer return the knife. He furiously scrubbed the handle with his sleeve and dropped it with a clunking thud.

Panicking, he couldn't leave with nothing. He delicately lifted two cold fingers from the table. He then whipped the badge out by the cord and slipped it in his trouser pocket.

Now more than ever he felt the urge to get as far away from there as possible. He headed for the natural light bleeding in from the hallway and rushed to the stained glass front door there, glancing back down at the tiles to check for a trail of red footprints.

The door was still ajar and rattled as he frantically wiped the Yale lock.

He put an eye to the crack in the door.

Outside, it was like nothing had happened, no hint of the horrors in there, just the chirp of distant birdsong and the swish of canopies along the tree-lined street in this sleepy Somerset suburb. Even the sun had come out.

Perhaps he could simply walk away from all this, pretend everything was okay again. But he knew the serenity wouldn't last for much longer. Soon, the place would be swarming with press and forensics, all eager to find out what the hell happened here.

When he heard another rattle of glass, he knew the unwanted visitor was still out the back. Now was his chance.

Fleeing a murder scene in broad daylight, Danny felt utterly exposed, as if he had to run from there naked. Silently, he slipped through the front door out into the squinting light.

CHAPTER 2

TWO MONTHS EARLIER

Danny felt the nerves creep up on him.

First-timer anxiety, he guessed, having oddly never even visited Doncaster racecourse let alone ridden there.

The more he tried to calm himself the sicker he felt. He knew he didn't just want this win, he needed it. But it was hard to be bullish given the current form of his yard.

Perhaps a good thing, he reasoned, as overconfidence led to expectation and pressure.

His mount, Gunslinger, was one of just two winners among a disappointing first crop of flat horses at Silver Belle Stables. He rated the chestnut colt as the brightest prospect, though that wasn't saying much as the only other with potential was the youngster Zebrawood, who'd yet to finish out of the front three in maidens.

Lately, he'd sent himself off to sleep thinking more about the jumpers in the yard, readying the likes of Welsh Champion Hurdler Powder Keg – who was set to have a sharpener later on this flat card – for the long winter ahead.

'Four to load,' the starter barked.

Danny's flushed cheeks tingled from a fresh crosswind. The bruised sky threatened yet more rain but all the wet had seemingly failed to dampen spirits among the Yorkshire crowd humming with anticipation in front of the grandstands some seven furlongs up track.

He was proud to be an ambassador for Cardiff's Ely Park which was currently attracting similar numbers though credit for the turnaround in fortunes there lay solely with the new racing manager and clerk of the course, Sophie Towers. He was just grateful for a local racetrack that had finally found a period of stability. He hoped for something similar for his yard.

His prep for the meeting had been a quick scan over the course map pinned to the jockeys' board in the Town Moor weighing room. He could see it was a fair track, suited to a straightforward horse that liked to find a stride and gallop right to the line. There were no jinks, or cutaways in the plastic rails to allow fast-finishers to nip up the inner, or pronounced undulations to knock a horse off its stride, or stiff uphill finish to catch out a trailblazer.

'A point and go track,' his old pal Stony would say.

Should suit mine, Danny thought, who'd won over a straight six at Nottingham. Being by Dante runner-up Fire Guard out of an Irish Oaks-third Velvet Glove, the step up to seven furlongs would also help.

Danny looked over at Nick Deeming, who was set to be crowned champion jockey in a ceremony later that afternoon. The striking blond, blue-eyed, was as popular with the public as he was in the weighing room, and the adoring press dubbed him Beckham of the jockeys. That was perhaps why his ride, the Jamie Bunce-trained Sweetshop, had been the subject of a major gamble since the morning, backed at all rates down from six-to-one into two-to-one.

The market plunge certainly wasn't based on form as the youngster had only won a slowly run Ely maiden and, even off a lowly eight stone and three pounds, appeared to be carrying too much weight to land this hot Class Two nursery – a valuable handicap for two-year-olds only.

In a handicap, each horse's ability is rated based on previous form and career profile, and is given a weight according to that rating, also known as a handicap mark. The greater the ability meant a higher handicap mark and therefore a bigger weight to shoulder in the form of lead plates held in a leather pouch under the saddle. A handicap mark can be adjusted up as well as down after each race, depending on how the horse performed.

In theory all horses in handicaps should cross the line together. But Danny knew better than most that racing wasn't an exact science and the gulf between theory and practice was widened by the inescapable truth that horses weren't machines and neither were the British Horseracing Authority – BHA – handicappers assigned to assess the handicap mark given to a horse.

Two of the heftier stall handlers eventually managed to convince Gunslinger forward into the stalls, much to Danny's relief. He hoped the youngster would be keener to leave them.

Cantering Gunslinger to the post he'd noticed the rails had moved slightly to take advantage of a fresh strip of unraced ground on the stands' side. The turf there had yet to be chewed and opened up for the rain to sink in.

Berthed in stall twelve of thirteen, Danny felt well placed to take advantage of this potential golden highway if able to grab it.

He tried to loosen the black armband from his silks. He hated feeling confined in any way. He couldn't wear a tie in his role as ambassador at Ely Park. Right now the armband felt more like one of those rubber cuffs to measure his raised blood pressure. He only kept it on in memory of stalwart dual-purpose trainer Larry Wallace, who'd been discovered in the red phone box in the betting ring in front of Ludlow grandstand three months ago. The post-mortem showed he'd been drinking and had been stabbed twice.

Apparently he'd remained in a coma until yesterday. Family were by his side when he slipped away, according to the new trade paper *The Racing Life*.

Danny had read the case was still open. Larry's wallet was found on him, cash inside. Just a mindless act of thuggery, police reckoned. No obvious motive as yet. No CCTV or DNA. No witnesses, probably as it happened after hours. Seemingly, the only witness who'd have been willing to testify was now dead.

'A win like this makes you glad to be alive,' were Larry's poignant last words to reporters in the winners' circle earlier that afternoon.

'Two to go,' the starter said, perched on his rostrum as he checked his watch again.

Already loaded up, Danny found himself peering between the grilles of his stall out on to the open expanse of lush turf covering the historic Town Moor ahead, home to the world's oldest classic – the St Leger.

The stalls shook noisily as the final horse, Sweetshop, loaded clumsily in to neighbouring stall thirteen.

He swiftly ran a reassuring hand down his colt's gleaming neck and neatly plaited mane. Wife Meg had won her twelfth best-turned-out as a groom in the paddock just minutes earlier.

All eyes were now on the starter who'd placed a hand over the release button on the panel of his rostrum.

The air was charged as silence descended; the quiet before the storm.

'All in,' called the starter, 'jockeys, ready!'

Danny's fingers tightened round the reins as the paddle doors of the stall sprung back with a metallic clunk. The grilles vanished.

He urged Gunslinger to fly from the gates and the youngster duly responded, effortlessly moving up through the gears. The extra practice in the replica stalls at home up in the Valleys had clearly paid off.

Passing the first of the red-and-white stripe furlong marker poles, he was relieved to find himself among the leaders. Although a race couldn't be won with a swift break, it can easily be lost with a slow one.

He also knew being in the front rank early gave him options: either ease off and get cover to help settle the colt or grab the fresh strip by the rails and try to make every yard.

Suddenly he felt Gunslinger pulling at the reins. He was lit up, doing too much in front. No way were they going to get home racing with the choke out on rain-softened ground.

Danny tugged on the reins enough for them to tuck in and get some cover behind the pacesetters.

Gunslinger soon settled down, knowing there was a wall of horse's rumps blocking his way.

He was moving nicely among the pack, protected by the buffering wind across this open track, as they galloped by the four-furlong pole.

With three furlongs to go, he could still feel there was plenty of horse under him as he started to look for a way out of the pocket.

When he saw an opening to his left, he was about to reluctantly switch away from the better ground nearer the rail. But it then shut as the leaders came together.

Two to go. Danny's glances became more frantic. He was trapped.

With every stride, Danny felt a growing sense of claustrophobia. And there was a clock in his brain counting down. He didn't want to be that unlucky loser.

As he pulled right on the reins to try to force a way out by the rail, he sensed a presence moving up on that side. Danny knew this would be his last chance to get a clear run. He wasn't going to be denied by a strong finishing rival darting up the rail. Danny held his ground as he edged across.

He heard a wail. 'Bastard!'

Glancing around, he saw Deeming's contorted face, not a look for the magazine covers.

He knew the press, the punters both on track and in the forums, and the stewards would also slate him for the reckless move. He grimaced inside but was willing to take the abuse if it meant he won the prize.

He pushed on as he could see the gap between the leader Catchall and the stand side rail shrink. He didn't want to be squeezed up and lose this, not after risking a riding ban.

He now wished there had been a cutaway with a false rail, or at least a bend where runners tended to fan out; anything to give him more space. He'd need to thread this opening with a surgeon's touch.

He went for it. The rail bent and shivered as his boot brushed the plastic. He sat lower and pushed harder. He could feel Gunslinger fill his mighty lungs and stretch his athletic legs to please his master, belying his age and experience.

Suddenly from the corner of his eye, he could see another leading rival, Spirit Animal, hit the front out in the centre of the track.

Passing the furlong pole, Danny knew it was now a match. He deftly snapped away his mud-spattered goggles and put his whip down. This horse was already giving his all.

But he still had to keep Gunslinger up to his work as Spirit Animal held a length advantage out wider.

Danny crouched even lower to reduce air resistance and blew hard as his arms and legs worked furiously.

Passing the half-pole, he had one-hundred-and-ten yards, or about six seconds, to make up the deficit, now just a half-length, a neck, a head, a short-head, a nose, a short-nose.

11

Danny saw the finish line and lunged forward as they flew by the lollipop stick, now a streak of red.

Head down! He didn't want to lose out for being camera shy in this photo.

'Boy, that's hard to call! One for the judge! Photo finish! Photo finish!' the race-caller blared over the speakers.

Danny had trouble easing up. It felt like Gunslinger could've gone round again.

When he finally galloped back towards the offshoot of black rubber tiles leading to the winners enclosure in front of the stands, he picked up on the crackle of nervous anticipation among the chattering crowd as the minutes passed.

The print must be close, Danny feared, just a pixel or two in it.

Suddenly, from nowhere, Deeming drew alongside. His gloved hand came up to shield his mouth from the TV cameras.

'You're finished! You were shit in your prime, now a has-been that needs to barge his rivals over to win,' Deeming growled.

'You were an unlucky loser, big deal. If I hadn't got up I would have been unlucky too for having to delay my run. It happens every day. We both had a shot at that gap and I made it first. That's racing,' Danny explained. 'If you can't get over it, you're in the wrong sport.'

'I did well to stay on the track let alone the horse. I don't care if you're a senior jockey, a fucking amateur wouldn't do that.'

'It's only a nursery,' Danny said. 'Anyone would think you'd backed yours.'

Deeming gave him an anxious look, as if concerned even an accusation might harm his brand.

The crowd fell eerily quiet as the dreaded chimes came over the speakers. 'Here is the result of the photograph for first place … first, number five Gunslinger, second, number three Spirit Animal and third, number twelve Sweetshop.'

Danny's hand punched the air. 'Yes!' escaped his lips.

'Lost fifty quid on the favourite 'cos of you,' shouted one middle-aged man clutching a betting ticket at the rail.

'Shouldn't be allowed on the road with that steering,' another cried.

He was surprised Sweetshop had found a second wind in time to make the frame in third place.

Perhaps the interference wasn't as bad as it seemed at the time, Danny hoped. Though it was more likely that Sweetshop had battled back well, given the way Deeming had taken the defeat just now.

'Stewards' enquiry, stewards' enquiry,' came over the speakers. 'The stewards will be looking into interference between the eventual winner and the third taking place between the two and one furlong markers. Please keep all tickets safe until the official result is declared, thank you.'

Danny didn't relish the prospect of facing the judges. He knew the race wasn't yet his if the stewards took the view that the result was definitely affected. He'd used his strength in the saddle to get up during the race and now he needed mental strength to keep it.

Beyond the paddock watchers standing on tiered steps surrounding the parade ring, queues had yet to form by the bookie boards.

Head lad Jordi led them into the winners circle to a smattering of applause. Aware of the camera, the swarthy Spaniard ran a hand over his thick black hair as he beamed a white smile up at Danny. He patted the neck and pinched an ear of the flashy chestnut colt. Jordi, too, clearly knew the importance of the race for the yard.

Yet the abuse kept coming from the paying public. 'You mugged me right off,' called out one. 'Will I get a refund in the post Rawlings? Sweetshop was running all over you. It was his gap.'

'Bastard cheat!' came another.

Danny found it hard to tune out the heckling as it was the abuse that stayed with him. As a former failed punter, he could relate to their frustration but it still hurt.

Ten minutes later, Danny emerged from the stewards' enquiry into the weighing room with a sore ear and a six-day ban for dangerous riding. However, nothing could have spoilt his mood. He'd come here for the win. Job done.

In the jockeys' changing room, he heard over the speakers, 'Result stands, weighed in, weighed in.'

He quickly peeled off his silk colours. He didn't want one of those hecklers identifying him by the brown and green colours.

He reckoned wife Meg was tending to the yard's star turn Powder Keg in the racecourse stables, who was entered for the one-mile two-furlong Listed Gillies Fillies' Stakes later on the card at two-fifty-five. As a stayer, the mare wasn't expected to win over such an inadequate trip but this still represented an ideal first spin for her before switching back to hurdles.

In his breeches, vest and back protector, he made his way by a small parade of stalls offering hot and cold drinks and food, handmade jewellery and crafts, and racing souvenirs, for those punters looking to spend their winnings. He continued to weave through the milling crowd at the rear of the main grandstand when he heard a woman's voice yell, 'Danny!'

Not another bad loser, Danny sighed.

He looked over and smiled.

'Sophie? Sophie Towers? Is that you?' he said playfully, still buzzing from the win.

He couldn't fail to recognise her really; she just looked very different out of work clothes.

With that shiny ink-black bob and a hugging Ferrari-red dress matching her lips, she looked like a femme fatale.

She didn't need to make this much effort. She had the face and figure of a model though she didn't seem to see it herself. Danny couldn't understand why she was still single.

'Married to the job,' appeared to be her stock answer whenever casually proposed by boozed-up admirers in the corporate tent at Ely Park.

He saw her as the saviour of that place.

'Young, bright and energetic – a breath of fresh air for a track sorely in need of it,' the local rag's editorial had commented after her appointment several months back.

And she'd certainly lived up to expectations, Ely Park was thriving.

'Didn't recognise you without the muddy sweatpants and a fork in your hand,' Danny said.

'You like,' she said, and gave him a twirl.

'You scrub up well,' Danny replied.

'I'll take that,' she said. 'Good as I'll get from you.'

'Feel like I should serenade you with some Chris de Burgh.'

She laughed. 'You're funny, Danny.'

Danny immediately clammed up. He was never good at taking compliments.

'Why are you here?' he asked.

'There's a gap between the final meeting of our Ely flat fixture list and the first over the jumps.' She leant in closer and added, 'Allows me to spy on how the big boys at the grade one tracks do it. It's nice to get away from Ely, like a holiday, albeit of the busman's variety.'

Suddenly her smiley face dropped slightly. She seemed to be distracted by something over Danny's left shoulder.

He turned and saw the hulking frame of trainer Jamie Bunce charging his way, face pinker than normal and ruffled shirt hanging half out. He looked like he'd come from the bar but definitely seemed to know where he was heading. Get revenge on the jockey that cost his horse Sweetshop the race, Danny feared.

Danny felt sure he wouldn't win this fight. There were about a dozen weight divisions between them. Probably do enough damage if he just ploughed on through him.

He looked back to warn Sophie to disappear but she already had. Danny wished he'd reacted as quickly.

With the press and TV crews never far away at such a high-profile meeting, Danny didn't want a scene and was about to try lose himself in the crowd too when he felt a hand grab him roughly by his bare arm and yank him out of Bunce's firing line with a bruising force.

From behind, Danny heard Bunce's booming voice shout as he charged, 'You! Get back here, fucking runt! Often have a runner down your joint Ely Park, so I'll be seeing you,' Bunce warned and with that, was gone as quickly as he'd appeared.

Danny was dragged past a suited doorman and into the glass foyer of the main Lazarus Stand.

'I can fight my own fights, mate,' Danny said, as he tried to get his bearings and composure back.

'Not this one, you can't,' came a reply.

CHAPTER 3

Danny had found some cover among punters pouring into the grandstand foyer, shaking umbrellas and leaving wet footprints as they went.

More than ever he was happy to keep a low profile, glad he'd somehow been removed from the situation out there before things got messy. He guessed it would be hard to figure out who was attacking who just from a still photo in tomorrow's *The Racing Life*. He knew not all publicity was good. Being caught up in a public brawl would make it even harder to attract new owners.

He stood there staring through the glass wall out at the paved concourse. Bunce would be hard to miss in the thinning crowd rushing to escape the sudden downpour, he hoped, probably saddling up a runner for the next race by now.

'Thank fuck for that,' Danny muttered to himself.

'It's not him you should be worried about,' came that voice again.

Danny turned, curious to see who had dragged him there to safety. He wanted to shake their hand and ask them why when others had just looked on.

His eyes flitted either side of a short, wiry old man wearing a saggy brown cardigan with matching corduroy trousers and brogues. He had purple tinted specs and wild grey hair like spun glass.

The laminated lanyard hung from his neck read: *Guest of the BHA – Howard Watkins – Flat Handicapper.*

'That was a rough race,' the man added.

Danny sighed. 'And I didn't expect the interference would keep going after the weigh in.'

'Lucky I was there, then.'

'Eh?' Danny replied. 'It was *you*?'

Danny's shoulders dropped slightly. Although he'd escaped physically unhurt, the same couldn't be said for his male pride. He'd been saved by a man old enough to be his father. He was now really glad the press hadn't arrived in time to witness it.

'Thanks,' Danny said begrudgingly. 'For what you did out there. Not many would come between Bunce in full flight. They don't call him the Bunsen Burner for no reason.'

'That was nothing.'

'Don't be modest,' Danny said.

'I wasn't,' Howard replied curtly. 'I was rather thinking about what they might do to you in the future. That, out there, would be *nothing* in comparison.'

'*They*?' Danny asked. 'What do you mean *they*?'

'I don't know who they are,' Howard snapped, as if angered by his own answer. 'But I'm close to finding out.'

'Maybe you should've got even closer before deciding to scare the hell out of me,' Danny said. 'Why are you even telling me this?'

'I want you to help me stop them.'

'Why don't you stop them?'

'I fear my days are numbered.'

Danny was getting the feeling Howard Watkins' intervention out there was no fortunate coincidence. 'Why am I in danger?'

'You stopped their horse,' Howard said.

'Sweetshop?' Danny asked. 'That was gamesmanship, part of race-riding. All's fair in love and racing. Anyway the stewards have already punished me.'

'You denied these people money.'

Danny recalled the monster gamble on the eventual third.

'Along with most of them out there,' Danny said. 'Did you hear the grief I got coming back in?'

'These are big money stakes,' Howard said. 'We're talking telephone numbers, not the tenner each-ways wagered by that lot.'

'Have you got inside info on this or something?' Danny asked, glancing again at the lanyard. 'Because the fact you're in the BHA is the only thing stopping me from leaving right now, as I would for any crank or loon.'

'I can't say, not yet,' Howard replied. 'But I can say that *they* will come for you.'

'Didn't Fred Archer say something similar?' Danny asked.

'And look what happened to him.'

Danny had read somewhere that the last words of the thirteen-times champion jockey – who many still regard as the best to ever ride – to his sister were 'Are they coming?' shortly before he shot himself in the head with a revolver.

'If you're worried about Bunce, he's a hothead, he'll soon simmer down,' Danny said, as if to convince himself more than anything. 'Unlike his jockey Deeming, he can get over an unlucky loser. He just spat his dummy out 'cos he didn't book me for the ride on Sweetshop. Mind, I'll probably leave calling a truce for today, feel in his current mood if I offer an olive branch, he'd snap it.'

'That's why I stepped in.'

'You shouldn't have, I can handle myself. The bigger they are the harder they—'

'Punch?' Howard interjected.

Danny didn't think he could go off his rescuer so quickly. Howard was beginning to freak him out more than Bunce, who at least was easy to read.

'Anyway, I'd best be off,' Danny said, pretending to check his watch. He was keen to meet up with Meg, who would be tacking up Powder Keg for the pre-parade ring.

'No!' Howard blurted. 'Please.'

Danny frowned. 'Look, thanks again, but I really—'

'Wait there.'

Danny watched as Howard's trembling hands fumbled in his cardigan pocket, seemingly even more shaken up by the events out there. He removed what looked like a crumpled newspaper cutting and handed it to Danny, who unfolded the paper.

It had been ripped from the front page of *The Racing Life*. The dot of the 'i' in *Racing* was the red circle on a finishing post. He read the headline: *Newmarket and Lambourn yards struck down by mystery illness.*

Danny looked up but Howard was now the one distracted by the glass wall.

He started to read the article. He'd heard some leading yards had already been struck down. It hadn't properly sunk in as he somewhat selfishly felt it didn't concern him, being safely stuck out in the depths of Glamorgan.

18

'What has this got to do with me?' Danny asked, folding the paper back up.

'Everything,' Howard said.

'I won a nursery handicap, for crying out loud,' Danny said. How could that be in any way linked to some equine illness spreading across the big training centres?

He tried to hand the article back.

'Keep it,' Howard replied, turning to eye Danny. 'As a reminder.'

'No offence but I kind of don't want reminding.'

'You will, in time.'

'Are you saying my yard is at risk?'

'Not just the yard,' Howard said. 'You are at risk.'

Danny was beginning to get really creeped out by the stranger.

'Did I get concussed out there or something 'cos none of this is making much sense.'

'I'm sorry to hear that, Danny,' Howard replied. 'At least I can say I tried.'

Danny sighed loudly. 'Anyway, kind of nice meeting you Howard,' he lied. 'I owe you a drink sometime … maybe.'

Howard said. 'At least take this,' he said.

'What is it?'

'My card,' Howard replied. 'If you suspect something, anything, report to me … this goes no higher.'

Suddenly a face appeared above Howard's left shoulder. A slim man, early-thirties with cropped black hair.

'Don't worry,' Howard said. 'He's one of us. Alex Park.'

Danny's shoulders relaxed.

'I've been sent to find you,' Alex said to Howard and then looked at Danny. 'Einstein here just can't be taken anywhere. Been sent down here to check he's not got lost.'

'Einstein?' Danny asked. 'It's the hair right?'

'The brains,' Alex replied. 'Meet our best numbers man.'

'Why are you handicappers here?'

'It's our BHA annual do to mark the end of the turf season on the flat,' Alex explained. 'The jumps boys take over the heavy work from here on, leaving just a few all-weather specialists to

19

keep the flat ratings updated until we return here for the Lincoln meeting in March. I can see you've met Howard, I'm so sorry.'

Danny tried not to smile. He didn't want to offend the man who'd bravely stepped in to defend him.

'I'm guessing you'll be the one needing a drink, then,' Alex added. 'Come on, the champers is all bought and paid for and will only go flat if it's not drunk. And some of us have already had their fill.' Alex looked at Howard again.

'I was just saying to … Howard here, I best be off, I'm working today.'

'Don't blame you,' Alex said. 'It's more like hard work up there. I've been to livelier wakes.'

The handicappers turned to leave. Danny suddenly felt unsettled, like he'd left an argument without having the last word. He had to find out more before he left. He quickly caught them up and waved his arm between the closing lift doors.

Wordlessly they rode the lift until it slowed to stop at the first floor.

Disappointingly, that's where Howard and Alex stepped out.

He followed them into a public hall running the length of the main grandstand.

'The petty cash float didn't stretch to a private box or suite on the upper floors, then,' Danny remarked.

Alex laughed and looked back. 'We were lucky to get free admission at the turnstiles. Gives you a chance to see how the other half live, Danny.'

'I'm no snob,' Danny replied. 'Just prefer somewhere less … public.'

He felt the anxiety grow as they weaved between several large circular tables crowded by groups of racegoers busy chatting, studying form and drinking. He appeared to be the only one there not having a good time.

He was acutely aware he was about to socialise with the very men who'd allotted him a weight low enough to win a race that saw him spoil a monumental gamble by knocking the favourite sideways.

He also knew racing was all about perception and this didn't look good.

It almost felt worse to be in there with just a mesh vest, body protector and breeches under his fleece. If he'd kept his silks on, he could have at least passed himself off as part of a stag do in fancy dress.

He zipped up his fleece some more and turned up the collar. He also made sure to lag a few paces behind the handicappers until they abruptly stopped by a bar table where a tall, lean man stood alone. He had grey-flecked hair and wore a tailored navy suit. His handsome forty-something face was clean-shaven, and his brown eyes were surprisingly sharp for a man standing by three champagne buckets. Also on the table, Danny noticed a folded copy of *The Racing Life*.

'Is this it?' Danny thought aloud.

'Sorry I'm a disappointment,' the man replied with a smile. 'Clive Napier, pleasure to meet you too, Danny.'

'I didn't mean you,' Danny replied, backtracking. 'I meant the turnout.'

Alex laughed. 'You can see now why I invited you up.'

'There are twelve handicappers currently working for the BHA,' Clive explained. 'Six assessing the Flat horses, while another six work on the National Hunt side.'

'So where are the other three flat handicappers?' Danny asked.

'No shows,' Alex replied. 'And there are four missing.'

'But you said there are six flat handicappers and there are three here.'

'Clive here doesn't count as one of the six,' Alex said. 'He's our boss.'

'There are thirteen handicappers in all each working with a particular class, race distance and age,' Howard explained. 'We all specialise in a particular group, helps us familiarise with certain set of horses, say three-year-old sprinters, over the course of the season.'

'All right, Howie, don't bore the lad, he's only just arrived, plenty of time for you to do that.'

In recent years, the BHA had partly lifted the veil on the ratings system. The handicappers were regularly seen discussing horses they'd marked on TV spots and in their own newspaper columns, particularly when the runners' weights are unveiled for high profile races, notably the Grand National. He guessed it was to give greater transparency to the often otherwise secretive world of racing, much like they did with the introduction of televised stewards' enquiries.

Alex began to pour champagne into a flute, mostly bubbles. 'There you go lad, get that down your neck, well deserved. I'll top it up once it's settled.'

'This'll do,' Danny said. 'Don't want to risk the drink-ride limit, not with Powder Keg coming up. Already felt the wrath of the stewards, once is enough for a day.'

'Congratulations, Danny,' Clive said. Their glasses clinked together to a chorus of 'cheers'.

Suddenly Danny felt the weight of eyes on them. If there was one thing worse than being seen with handicappers, he reckoned, it was being seen celebrating with them.

He nervily glanced around. But no one was actually looking.

'Relax Danny, we're off duty and you've had a winner,' Alex said.

He was right. Danny needed to keep calm in the build up to Powder Keg's run. 'What made you all get into handicapping?'

'I had a career in the City, but found the lure of my first love too great,' Alex explained and put an arm round Howard. 'This one was in it before I was born. One of a kind, he's like a human calculator, which, thinking about it now, kind of makes him obsolete since the invention of the calculator.' Howard frowned. 'And Clive here was demoted from another department within the BHA.'

'I switched, I was never demoted,' Clive said and then turned to Danny. 'You certainly know how to win at all costs.'

He seemed keen to steer the conversation away. It was clearly a sore topic.

'I'm beginning to wish I hadn't,' Danny said, and felt a kick against his riding boot from Howard's side.

Howard's words in the foyer came back in a flash. 'Report to me … this goes no higher.'

Danny guessed that included his boss, Clive Napier. It was his turn to hastily change topics. 'Makes a nice change to win away from my local track, Ely Park.'

'That was such a shame,' Howard said.

'What is?'

'Haven't you heard?' Howard asked.

'Howard, don't,' Clive ordered.

'Ely will soon be shutting its gates for the final time.'

Danny's confused smiled soon vanished when he could see from the other faces that this was no joke.

'I'd heard about some proposed plans for a housing estate there but I knew it was never going to get by your lot at the BHA or the Ely board members. Probably just some greedy developer trying it on. Tell me this is just a wind up, right?' Danny asked but was met by silence. 'Right?!'

'It's classified,' Clive said.

'It *was* classified,' Danny snapped. 'And now I know, so tell me what the fuck you know.'

Danny felt his heart thud against the padded body protector.

'I'm an ambassador to that track,' Danny added, downing the rest of the bubbly. He felt like smashing the glass. 'My yard depends upon it being open. The travelling costs to tracks like this are crippling. What have you heard?'

'The council needs housing close to the city apparently, not brown belt land further out,' Howard said, 'and with the Ely station newly built, there's the infrastructure ready to go.'

'Whose side are you on?' Danny snapped. 'Anyway, that platform's to serve the track, like it did when Cardiff races was first there a century ago.'

'Do you honestly think the council would build a station for a racetrack?' Howard said. 'Most councillors would see horseracing as a folly for the rich, rather than a social necessity. A waste of land that could go to help address the housing shortage in the city.'

'You're telling me the housing was already greenlit before the station was?'

'None of this has gone public and until then—' Clive said and then shook his head witheringly at Howard, who'd just opened his mouth again. 'Don't!'

'Hang on, this must be bullshit, I just met the clerk of the course there, Sophie Towers, she turned that place around, she's one in a million. The track doesn't even need pop concerts after racing to fill the stands. That place is her life. It's the child she's yet to have, so she'd have been in mourning now, yet she never mentioned the sale being rubberstamped once out there,' Danny explained. 'In fact, she was on top form just now as if it was business as usual. She's even picking up tips here to improve the track for the *future*.'

'Perhaps she's in denial, like you are,' Howard said.

'Or got a new job,' Alex said. 'As you say, she's one in a million. And Howard, you could've broken it to him easier. It's his local track, and mine for that matter. I live not far from there, in Penarth. Love going to that place. But it'll hit you a lot harder, Danny, I'm sure.'

'You can understand why I'm having trouble getting my head round this, Ely puts on racing for the flat and jumps all year round and could take more fixtures if your lot at the BHA would grant them.'

'Don't blame us,' Clive said. 'Every track is after more fixtures, doesn't necessarily make them a viable business.'

'Or give them a divine right to survive,' Howard said.

'But don't you see, it's made good money over the summer.'

'Not enough money to brush off an offer from a developer it seems,' Howard said.

'The board of directors wouldn't allow this,' Danny said. 'The area needs it as an attraction, and for local jobs, including mine!'

'If it's happened there before,' Howard said. 'It can happen again.'

'That was different, the track was failing when it shut there in the Thirties,' Danny said, recalling the first track at Cardiff.

'It's not all bad news,' Howard said.

'How is Ely shutting not bad news?' Danny asked.

'Racing will be lucky to see the spring,' Howard replied.

'Shall we see if that's in the news, Howard?' Danny asked and picked up *The Racing Life* from the bar table.

His hands were now shaking with rage. He stopped thumbing the pages when he saw one had been crudely torn away. Page nine. Danny suspected it was the continuation of the article on the front page now folded in his pocket.

Danny kept turning the pages sarcastically to make sure no one there knew he'd noticed. It seemed Howard coming down there really wasn't merely a coincidence. He'd clearly ripped the relevant article out and headed down there as soon as he'd seen Danny badly hamper Sweetshop.

'Keep your voice down, Danny,' Clive said and swiped the newspaper away. 'There isn't a thing anyone here can do about Ely.'

'I don't believe a word of that,' Danny said. 'How can the rulers of the sport give the green light to killing off one its success stories?'

'Believe what you like, it'll be made public soon enough,' Clive said. 'And don't think that racing will die. Howard likes to embellish things, he's drunk.'

'I'm not a drunk!' Howard cried.

Clive turned. 'Alex, take that booze off him. I said you were drunk, not *a* drunk. There's a huge difference.'

Just then, Danny saw Jordi weaving the tables towards them. This time there was fear in his eyes.

'Danny!' Jordi cried.

Danny knew something wasn't right for his head lad to have addressed him by his first name and not Mr Rawlings. This was a widely accepted tradition in racing yards as a mark of respect from stable staff to their boss.

The last time he'd heard Jordi call him Danny was at the yard's Christmas do.

Danny felt a hand prod his fleece. He turned to see an old lady in a floral dress and specs.

'Would you sign this for my grandson over there? He's a big fan but he's shy bless him.' She then looked closer and frowned, pulling the racecard away. 'Oh. You're not Nick Deeming.'

Danny was flattered he'd been mistaken for a jockey several years younger, though the thickness of her specs kept him grounded.

'Are you a leading jockey?'

'If I was, would you need to ask?'

'There's no need to be like that, young boy,' she said, and stomped off muttering, 'How very rude!'

25

Right now Danny didn't have the time or patience to make amends. The Nick Deeming fan club was large enough, he reasoned.

'What is it?' Danny asked Jordi, though not really wanting an answer.

'It's Megan.'

Danny glanced over at Howard, who was staring at Jordi as if waiting on an answer too.

'What's happened?'

'Sorry, I don't know,' Jordi said, voice shaky, 'but please, come quick, she cries.'

Danny gave Howard a look.

They will come for you.

Danny put his empty glass down and headed for the lift without saying another word to the handicappers.

He stepped in and held the door open for Jordi.

'Where is she?' Danny asked Jordi, voice quieter and softer not to create a scene among others in the confines of the lift.

'The stables,' Jordi said.

When they stepped out of the lift, Danny's pace quickened, fuelled by adrenaline.

A growing concern for his wife mixed with alcohol on an empty stomach was a sickly cocktail.

Passing the clock tower of the Lazarus stand, Danny glanced back. He saw Howard talking with Jordi. They were in deep conversation when he saw Jordi slip what looked to be a brown paper package into his blue fleece.

What the hell was going on?

Danny supressed the urge to stare. He quickly looked ahead again, towards the stables where he was heading. He didn't want either of them to know he'd seen the exchange. His head lad was already on a final warning for turning up late more than once and slacking on the job. Jordi didn't know that the final warning was there more as a deterrent; he couldn't afford to sack the most experience member of the team, particularly now the yard was an all-year-round operation with both jumpers and flat horses.

Why did Howard say racing would be lucky to see the spring?

Danny could see by the intense look in his eye that this was more a moment of clarity than just drunk-talk.

He pictured the torn page now scrunched in his pocket.

Was the mystery illness gripping Newmarket and Lambourn about to spread further afield?

Were *they* infecting or poisoning the horses?

As he turned into the stabling, he saw Meg wiping her big eyes. She ran to him and gave him a hug. Danny didn't know who was comforting who. He didn't want to let go of her warm body.

'Are you okay, Meg? You're scaring me.'

'I'm okay,' she sobbed.

'Then what's wrong?'

'It's Kegsy, she's fallen ill.'

'What do you mean? She was fine in the van on the journey up,' Danny said. 'You mean she might not race?'

She released herself from the embrace, enough to face him, though she can't have seen much through those wet eyes. 'She might not live.'

Danny looked over at Howard, who'd been stopped from entering the secure stables by a guard. He swore he saw Howard mouth, 'They will come for you.'

'Seems they already have,' escaped Danny's lips.

CHAPTER 4

Danny stared up at the five furlongs of dirt, right to the wooded copse near the ridge at the peak of Silver Belle Estate where stable lass Beth Jenkins stood primed with a stopwatch.

The sky was like a paint sampler, turning lighter shades of blue every time he checked.

The mists had been all but burnt off by the weak winter sun yet it still felt like there was a heavy cloud stuck over the yard. During the weeks since Doncaster, one by one his horses had joined Powder Keg in the old part of the stabling, which had now become better known as the sick bay.

'And then there were two,' Danny mumbled.

'Two what?' Meg asked.

Danny laughed. 'My entire string is out here on the gallop strip.'

'What's funny about that?'

'Nothing,' Danny sighed, still craving the comfort and safety of his warm bed. 'Thought it would be better than crying.'

'You okay? It's normally me that hates mornings.'

'Just the usual hysteria setting in.'

He kept his mobile on in hope of receiving news of test results from the vet. The first set of blood samples had come back inconclusive, similar to the yards in the newspaper article Howard gave him. The waiting was the worst part.

The deputy head of the handicappers had left him spooked by more questions than answers.

It made no sense to him that the BHA would green-light the sale of Ely Park. And what had Howard told Jordi as his head lad pushed a brown paper parcel into his fleece?

He looked across. He could see her white breath as she tugged on her leather riding gloves. Her eyes were puffy. She'd barely slept since Powder Keg had been struck down by the illness. Danny was the same now the yard was in virtual lockdown. The costs of ownership from equine dentists' fees, physios, vets, farriers, specialist feeds and staff all still needed paying whether the horses were racing or not, yet all bar two of the horses were currently on discounted box-rest rates as a goodwill gesture to owners, rather than the higher full-training fees. And with most of the horses resting and losing fitness by the day there was little hope of a share of any prize money any time soon, which all meant the yard currently ran at a loss.

His stomach tightened. This was no ordinary gallop. It felt like the morning of a school exam, not that he'd been to many.

He was sitting on the juvenile colt Zebrawood, though he knew there was a lot more riding on the colt in this gallop. The striking bay youngster had been sent to him by self-made multimillionaire Garrick Morris as a trial horse to test Danny's skills as a trainer, along with the note, 'Deliver on Zebra and this is just the start'. Garrick, a proud Welshman, was reportedly keen to back a yard in his homeland.

Zebrawood had been rated seventy-eight by the handicappers after finishing in the frame in maidens at Sandown, Goodwood and Newmarket for his previous trainer. 'Clearly a winner waiting to happen,' was the comment by a form analyst in The Racing Life. Off a very fair mark, Danny was confident they were right. Being an early January foal, he also held an age advantage at this stage over most other two-year-olds. It was like at school where those born at the start of the academic year held an advantage over those scraping in with a birth date at the end, almost a year younger yet treated by teachers and exam boards as the same.

Meg was on Pobble Beach, who earned a mark of sixty-six after winning an Ely maiden in a slow time.

As a rule of thumb over five furlongs, a three-pound higher handicap mark converts to a horse's length superiority at the finish up where Beth stood patiently. The handicappers had therefore assessed that the twelve-pound higher Zebrawood was entitled to beat Pobble Beach by four lengths off level weights here. Anything less convincing would suggest he'd struggle on the racetrack off his current mark. And if unable to even pick up a handicap, Danny knew deep down he'd have failed the trial horse and Garrick would look to another Welsh yard to bankroll.

Danny was convinced that if Zebrawood made the grade it would rocket Silver Belle Stables into the big league.

His stomach tightened some more.

'Are we doing this or what?' Meg asked. 'Beth's thumb will be getting cramp over the timer.'

'On three,' Danny said. 'And remember, don't go easy on yours just to let me get the result I want.'

'Yeah, yeah, leave everything out here, blah, blah,' Meg whined.

'I just want to see how good Zebrawood is.'

'Don't worry, I won't hold back.'

He knew Meg would give her all. Her ruthless side only came out in dance competitions and races.

Several strides in Danny realised she wasn't kidding. Pobble Beach had quickly gained the upper hand, turning a half-length advantage into a length, then a length and a half.

He reacted by quickly slotting in behind to cut down on air drag. But two furlongs into the gallop, he could see Meg had extended the lead further.

He began to sit lower and row harder to try claw back the deficit but it was clear Meg and Pobble Beach had already gone, along with any gains from slipstreaming them.

He still asked Zebrawood for more. He didn't want to give the horse the excuse of easing down. He knew the result was bad. He needed to know just how bad.

But Zebrawood simply had nothing more to give. His trial horse only appeared to have the one pace and that was slow.

Up ahead, he saw Beth press the timer round her neck as Meg flew by her on the other side of the plastic rail.

Beth looked down and frowned. It didn't make Danny feel any better. If the time clocked by Meg was slow, he dreaded to think what it meant for the measure of Zebrawood's ability.

Flashing by Beth, Danny could see Pobble Beach's backside and Meg were about four lengths up. He'd expected a wide margin winner this morning but definitely not in that order.

There was a worrying lack of excuses. Zebrawood hadn't lost his stride or suffered interference and the vet had given this pair a clean bill of health having scoped clean just an hour earlier.

Shock quickly turned to disappointment then frustration.

'Perhaps my one is a star,' Meg said when she saw the look on Danny's face. They turned at the top of the ridge.

'You saw the shite race your one bagged at Ely,' Danny said.

'We'll find a race for Zebrawood.'

'Sellers and claimers won't register with a man like Garrick,' Danny explained. 'He didn't become rich by dealing with low graders. We need to get a handicap win out of him at the very least.'

Danny knew Meg was optimistic to a fault. He didn't have the heart to remind her that all bar two were currently on reduced fees and would take time to get back in full training which meant the yard was off the media radar and currently making a loss.

He asked, 'Beth, what time did we clock?'

Beth's cheeks glowed.

'Don't be shy, it can't get any worse than that gallop.'

'I didn't clock a time.'

'What?!' Danny snapped, pinching the bridge of his nose.

'You heard her,' Meg said.

'You only had one job,' Danny replied. He'd never failed to clock a time as gallop watcher years back. He knew timing a race was a big part in form analysis and a major factor the BHA handicappers call upon to assess lightly raced horses. 'The clue is in the name, it's a *stop*watch … you have to stop the bloody thing.'

'I did,' Beth cried. 'Trouble is, I never started it.'

It explained the look of dread on Beth's face as she looked to the timer at the end of the gallop. Like head lad Jordi, Beth was also on a final warning. At least Jordi had a plausible excuse, of being homesick, missing the sun, family and lifestyle of Spain. Beth was a local lass, born and bred.

But deep down he knew he couldn't sack her either; they needed a skeletal staff even when the horses were out of full training and she had stayed loyal to the yard when others left due to poor pay or long hours.

'What good will you do taking it out on Beth?' Meg asked.

Danny turned. He knew it would be two against one if he wasted time arguing up here. And nothing could reverse the outcome of the gallop. Wordlessly he trotted Zebrawood back down to the stabling.

Galloping into the chilly morning air had woken him up but right then he'd rather have stayed in bed and not faced the sobering

31

truth that Garrick had sent him a dud. His main hope of a fresh injection in bloodstock was clearly rated too high to be a success in handicapping. He was only glad he hadn't invited Garrick to watch the gallop. There was only so far patriotism would stretch, particularly for a hard-nosed businessman who'd not made his money by being charitable.

But he knew worse things can and do happen, namely driving home with an empty horse box. All the other horses were currently ill but stable and comfortable. That still didn't stop him wanting to kick the outside wall of the new stabling block as he walked by. He wished he'd now put up a punch bag in one of the spare empty loose boxes.

It's not as if he had any training or qualifications to make a change in career and he was no longer the bright young hope on the racing scene. All he knew was riding and training horses, aside from a brief spell as a form adviser for a betting syndicate.

The empire he'd spent years building up was crumbling all around. Even the stable staff had started to fail him.

As he led Zebrawood back into the stable block, the colt seemed disappointingly chipper, ears swivelling like satellite dishes, bright eyed and feet on springs. Danny was desperate to find an excuse for the poor display. There was no heat in either his fore or hind legs.

Heavy footed, Danny sloshed through the chemical footbath, entering the new part of the stables, now a quarantine area.

Circling the stable courtyard, Danny barely noticed a wheelbarrow on the shale gravel in the middle. He'd seen Jordi pushing it around earlier. There was a pitchfork leaning against the barrow.

Danny was too distracted to be annoyed by the fact his head lad had left a sharp tool out. He consoled himself that the barrow was no longer brimming with hay. At least he'd put down fresh bedding.

He made sure Zebrawood was settled in his box. The bay's white face and shiny ebony eyes came bobbing back over the V of the stable door as Danny bolted it shut. He pinched the colt's ear and gave him his last mint.

'You're a handsome devil aren't you, boy – I can see why Garrick fell for you at the sales, just wish you were as good as you look. Perhaps it's just been an off day for us all, eh, boy?'

An icy gust of wind blow over them both. What if the illness was airborne?

He couldn't afford for either of the two left in the quarantine area to move on to the sick bay. And unlike the top trainers, he didn't have a satellite yard to truly separate the sick from the well.

He picked out Sophie Towers from the contact list on his mobile.

'Sophie? Hi, it's Danny,' he said. 'Yeah, not so bad. What it is – you know that favour you owe me, well I was wondering … can I take a couple of mine to stay at the racetrack stabl—'

Danny stopped when he heard the rustle of hay in the neighbouring loose box. 'You okay to wait a sec, Soph?'

He put his hand to the phone. He glanced over at the empty wheelbarrow and called to the half-open stable door. 'Hello? Jordi? You in there?' Silence. Danny turned back to the phone. 'Can I call you back, Soph?'

He turned off his phone. There was another rustle, and he swore he'd seen a black shape move inside. The box was meant to be empty and was due a steam clean.

They will come for you.

He now saw that pitchfork as a potential weapon.

Danny rushed over and raised the fork, trembling prongs pointing at the stable door.

'Who is it?' Danny called out, thankful of the deeper early morning voice. There was a groan from inside. 'I know you're in there!'

Suddenly, a man's fleshy face appeared in the top half of the doorway, far enough for the light to catch his features.

'No,' Danny whispered in disbelief, slack wrist lowering the fork, prongs clattering the shale. 'It can't be.'

'It can,' came a gruff reply. 'It's good to see you again, Danny.'

CHAPTER 5

'Gash?!' Danny cried. For a moment, he shut his eyes as if searching for some inner peace. 'This just gets better and better.'

'I knew you'd be pleased to see me.' Gash clearly hadn't picked up on the sarcasm, or hadn't wanted to.

'I presumed you'd be in a gutter someplace by now.'

'You were nearly right,' Gash said and shook his head like a wet dog to shed bits of straw from his greasy black hair and stubbly face. 'I've stayed in nicer.'

'You've been there all night?'

'Well, you didn't want a knock on the door at that hour,' Gash replied. He snapped his neck. 'Wish I'd packed a travel pillow now.'

'This isn't a bloody hotel,' Danny said in a strangled whisper, not to upset the inquisitive Zebrawood, who was looking across at Gash's head poking from next door. 'What the hell are you doing here? After all these years, I'd just about forgotten you and all the things you did.'

'I can understand, it's a shock me turning up like this,' Gash said, showing his palms. 'I didn't want to be here either. I'm just down on my luck and I didn't have a friend to turn to.'

'Wonder why that is.'

'You're every right to be angry with me. I let you down, but I'm a changed man now.'

'And so am I,' Danny replied. 'I'm no longer the green, gullible fool that trusted leeches like you. You deserve a smack, not a freebie.'

'And you're right, I'd deserve it,' Gash said. He stuck out his cheek. 'Hit me if it makes us even.'

'Nothing would make us even, Gash, and I'm not that kind of man. My family is my life now. And spare me the Mr Nice Guy routine, it only makes me more suspicious of what you're wanting from me after all this time.'

'A room … for the night,' Gash replied. 'That's all, I'll even sleep in one of these, despite the smell.'

'It's called a loose box. No wonder you blew the betting syndicate money I'd spent years building up. You don't know one end of a horse from the other.'

'I took some hay from the barrow there, I hope you don't mind, it felt like fresh sheets. Never thought I'd be so excited by some straw.'

'I'm glad you enjoyed your stay,' Danny replied facetiously, 'but it's time to check out and sod off, we need to steam clean the box.'

Gash smelt both his armpits.

'The yard is in virtual lockdown because of illness.'

Gash stepped from the box. 'That's all I need.'

'Equine illness, you're a different animal and won't catch it … sadly. But you might spread it.'

'I can't go.'

'Why the hell not?'

'I've got nowhere to go.'

'Book a hotel in Cardiff,' Danny said. 'There'll be loads of empty rooms this time of year.'

'I've no money.'

'You haven't changed in every way then,' Danny said.

Gash fished out his smartphone and tapped the shiny screen. 'Look.'

'I don't want see your bank account.'

'It's not,' Gash replied. 'Come over, see.'

'You come here.'

'Not while you're pointing that thing.'

Danny propped the fork back up against the barrow.

Gash handed the phone over. Danny held it by the fingertips, like lifting a filthy rag.

'It's okay, it's been safely in my pocket.'

'I know,' Danny said, 'That's what I'm worried about.'

Danny's eyes skated up and down a long list of betting transactions with columns showing the different stakes, selection, time. There was also a win/loss column which was largely filled with L's outnumbering the W's.

'That's my betting account,' Gash said.

'Still a prized loser I see,' Danny said. 'Doubt there's any danger of this bookie limiting your stakes, every cloud and all that.'

'I'm more profitable to them than those betting machines are to the shops. If they heard I'd run out of money, it would probably shake their stock value.'

'You've only got yourself to blame, and you're showing me like it's a badge of honour.'

'I'm not proud, I'm ashamed. You had the same problem, we've got that in common at least.'

'You have a funny idea about bonding,' Danny said. 'Why should I care?'

'Look, I wasn't going to lay it all out there, but I turned to gambling as a distraction to numb myself when my dad died. I lost all the inheritance and now I'm stuck.'

'I know what you're trying to do,' Danny said. 'Playing every hand to try to soften me up. You knew my dad was dead last time we worked together and you also knew how much he meant to me. This is your cheap way of getting me to feel for you. Well, it won't work. You're father's probably not even dead.'

'Kick a man when he's down, why don't you,' Gash said. 'I can't get a job though I've tried. My CV is as empty as my wallet, just has my name and school exams on it and I could only pass four of them. I've been a placer all my life, putting bets on for others, like when we were colleagues, you as a form student, me as the middleman, we made a good team right? We could spend nights here reliving the good old days.'

'They might be old but they weren't good.'

'Just one more then and I'll be gone, never seen again. Just imagine that.'

'Oh trust me, I already have,' Danny said. He handed the phone back. 'Now make it happen.'

'What if I refuse to?'

Danny knew Gash held a big weight advantage and there was bound to be some strength behind that flabby frame. He'd struggle to shift Gash off his land if he didn't want to go and would no doubt be back the next night if he did. He had an idea.

'Look, I'll go ask the missus.'

Gash nodded. 'At least I've got a chance that way, I guess. How is Sara? Pass on my love, would you?'

'It's Meg now.'

'Oh, I'm sorry it didn't work out.'

'I'm not,' Danny said, 'I wouldn't have met Meg then.'

'Well, pass my love on anyway,' Gash said. 'It'll be good to meet the new Mrs Rawlings.'

'In your dreams,' Danny mouthed, walking away.

No way Meg would allow a stinking stranger in their family home, Danny reckoned.

He knew he was passing on responsibility but it was clear Gash wasn't going to take a 'no' from him.

Walking back to the yard, Danny composed and sent a text to Sophie that read: *Soph, got cut off when about to ask if 2 of mine can stay in racecourse stables until lab results get back. Big favour in return, I promise! Ta, Danny.*

He walked the path that led to the shadowy rear of the trainer's lodge – a three-bed, red-bricked cottage that once housed the groundsman when Silver Belle Estate was owned by the Samuel family.

About to open the kitchen door out the back, he was distracted by some movement in his periphery.

Danny stopped and looked across. He saw Jordi, who was pacing head, bowed across, the tarmacked area, heading away from the large store barn towards the lines of practice fences and schooling ring.

Even from there, Danny could see he'd left the barn door open. That place was out of bounds to all staff without prior permission from either Danny or Meg.

He didn't know what was more concerning, the fact his head lad had entered or that he'd left without locking up, literally an open invite to gangs of thieves in the area, according to the local TV news.

What the hell was he doing in there?

He was about to shout over but reckoned he wouldn't get an honest answer. He pictured Jordi sliding the brown paper package inside the yard's fleece walking beside Howard at Doncaster. What was he being paid to do? Was it linked to the sudden sickness gripping the yard?

Danny waited for Jordi to disappear round the other side of the lodge, probably slinking off, with no more lots to tack up or bedding to spread.

Danny rushed over and poked his head inside the barn. He flicked on the strip lights high above.

Everything seemed to be in its jumbled place. Amid the chaos were grass cutters, plastic rails for the gallop strip and schooling ring, replacement fences and hurdles, feed bags and firewood for the lodge.

He was about to flick the switch off when he heard the metallic clunk of something crashing to the floor somewhere deep in there.

Instinct made Danny recoil. He then stood mannequin-like as he scanned the barn, heart pounding his rib cage.

'Hello?' he called out.

Danny waited in the eerie silence. When he glanced back he saw the metal barn door was banging the frame in the wind. He smiled. The sound must've bounced off the walls.

He was about to turn when he noticed one of the feedbags looked different to the others. Up close, he saw there was a tear in the clear plastic.

Had the feed been got at? That would explain why the first test results had come back inconclusive for all known infections and diseases.

Was Jordi poisoning the horses?

Danny felt dirty even considering the prospect. But he had been spending less time with the string of jumpers and Flat racers and no animal lover would leave a pitchfork out in a working yard.

Perhaps Jordi's motive was in the paper package he'd been given by Howard at Doncaster.

Danny scooped up a handful of feed. It smelt of corn, oats, barley and ground grass mix, nothing chemical about it.

Just in case, he dragged the bag away to separate it from the others. He stopped himself from chucking the contents on to the compost heap as he suspected it might be needed as evidence against Jordi and Howard further down the line. He reckoned he ought to send a sample to the vet, or get a toxicology report.

However hard it was to think of Jordi as the enemy within, Danny had to face up to the possibility, as he locked up behind him and went to find Meg in the cottage.

Outside the kitchen, he slipped off his chemical-smelling boots and left them to air.

He went from the kitchen to the lounge where he saw Meg facing the fireplace.

'Meg, there you are, I need you to say 'no' to something,' Danny said as he entered.

He stopped in the doorway when he also saw Gash was also stood near the hearth, elbow leaning against the mantelpiece as he nursed a large whisky.

'Need you to say no?' Gash interjected in a posher voice, more refined and less threatening to his normal one, and his little finger stuck out as he cradled the tumbler. All that was missing was a cravat and smoking jacket.

'Jesus,' Danny said. 'Why did you let him in?'

'It doesn't sound like I'd have had a fair trial, Danny. It's a jolly good job I was invited in.'

'Are you going to be a pig all morning, Danny? He was freezing, *and* he's your friend,' Meg said and raised a slightly faded Polaroid in her hand. Danny recognised himself with Gash stood alongside on the gallops somewhere, probably Newmarket or Lambourn.

'He's Photoshopped it, no way would I be smiling in a photo with his arm round me,' Danny said and turned to Gash. 'And I told you to wait out there.'

'So you do know each other, then,' Meg said.

'We go way back, don't we Danny? Oh, the stories we could tell you,' Gash said.

'I can imagine,' Meg said, grinning.

'Mind, I better not reveal all, you don't want another divorce on your hands, Danny.'

Meg's grin dissolved.

'When I said earlier you'd done well for yourself, I didn't reckon upon this well,' Gash added, as if trying to get her back onside. 'It seems there's brains *and* beauty in this marriage, both on her side.'

Danny looked to Meg for a response, expecting an eye roll at the very least, but the grin had returned.

Meg said, 'It'll be fun hearing all the old stories. You must have loads. It's nice to finally meet a friend more his own age,' Meg said. 'He never talks about his past.'

Thanks, mother, Danny groaned.

'Always been a dark horse, our Danny,' Gash said with a knowingly look. 'Oh, I could tell you a few things that would make you blush.'

Meg fought off a laugh. Danny could she was loving this, payback for his outburst at Beth on the gallops.

'We can take on the drinks cabinet with no more gallop work tomorrow,' she said.

'Looks like someone already has,' Danny said, glaring at the whisky in Gash's hand.

'Poor thing was trembling from sleeping rough,' Meg said.

'It's medicinal,' Gash added.

'At this hour?'

'My dear late mother—'

'Oh, she's dead 'n all is she?'

'Danny!' Meg fumed.

'It's okay, Meg, I'll be strong,' Gash said hammily. 'As I was saying, my mother used to tell me, anything after eight is acceptable.'

'In the morning?' Danny asked.

'If you insist,' Gash said raising his glass. 'Cheers.'

'That better not be the thirty-year-old good stuff I've been saving for special occasions,' Danny snapped.

'This is a special occasion,' Meg said and gave him a look. 'Isn't it, Danny.'

Danny was too angry to find the words.

'I'd ask for a refund,' Gash said, as he rested the empty tumbler on the mantelpiece. 'Bit harsh on the gullet for me, I find.'

'How did you find us? Meg asked.

'And why now?' Danny added.

'I saw you win a race at Doncaster on one of the main channels on telly a few weeks back.'

Danny groaned. He didn't want reminding.

'What's wrong?' Gash said.

40

'He feels it's a cursed win,' Meg explained.

'Why would a win be a curse?' Gash asked.

''Cos nothing's gone right since,' Danny said, 'including now.'

'You were my last resort,' Gash explained, 'if that makes you feel any better.'

'Why would being a last resort make me feel better, even coming from you?'

'Ignore him, Gash, he's had a bad morning, that's all.'

Danny phone bleeped. He read the text.

Both Meg and Gash looked at him.

'Just work,' Danny said. 'Meg, can we talk?'

'Later,' Meg said. 'Sorry about Danny, he's never been the best host.'

'You really don't want this, Meg, trust me,' Danny said.

'Gash has been nothing but a charming man.'

'He can't even be trusted to stay out there,' Danny argued.

'You were taking forever,' Gash slurred.

'I had to check up on something,' Danny said.

'While he was freezing out there?' Meg questioned.

'I couldn't wait,' Gash explained. 'I didn't want a character assassination.'

'Shame you didn't do the same when I needed backing up in court on trial for murder,' Danny snapped. That felt surprisingly good to get off his shoulders. It had clearly been festering all this time. 'You see, Gash was the go-between for me as a work watcher and form analyst, and the wealthy backers of a betting syndicate,' Danny told Meg. 'But here's the rub, this one refused to show up at court to show I was of good character and if that wasn't enough, he blew the syndicate funds. I had hoped to go to the grave without crossing paths with him again. Not much to ask is it?'

'I was a selfish young man, that much is true,' Gash said. He came over and offered a hand. 'Sorry, old friend.'

'Everyone deserves a second chance,' Meg said. 'Now shake his hand, Danny.'

Danny just wanted to escape in the van with the horses.

'She's a rare one, all right,' Gash said. 'Don't let her out of your sight.'

He then started scratching his back.

'You must be feeling proper grubby, poor thing,' Meg said. 'You'll find clean towels in the airing cupboard if you'd like a shower. Danny's clothes won't fit, but you can borrow the baggy dressing gown he never wears while I get those clothes washed.'

'Thanks, Mrs Rawlings,' Gash said.

'Anytime, and it's Meg.'

Gash disappeared upstairs.

Danny waited to hear the creak of floorboards on the landing.

'Seriously, if all this is to get me back for shouting at Beth, we're more than even,' he said, ''Cos believe me, he's no friend of mine.'

Meg picked up the Polaroid.

'That's a snapshot and you're ordered to smile for it. Like New Year's Eve, forced fun, the lot of it,' Danny said. 'Oh, and he's skint, gambled away whatever money he had.'

'How do you know that?'

'He showed me his online betting account.'

'All the more reason to let him stay. You were in a similar fix to him years back, no?'

'Yeah,' Danny admitted. 'But if you let him stay, he'll just disappear into the night, along with anything worth taking here.'

'I reckon you're still pissed off about the gallop. He seems genuinely nice. A bit on the smelly side, but he's sorting that.' She glanced up at the ceiling towards the distant sound of gushing water.

'You won't be so keen when you hear he wants to stay a few nights,' Danny said, trying a different tack.

Suddenly Jack came in crying, 'Mammy, mammy.'

The checked sleeve of his shirt was up far enough to show a small red graze on his forearm.

Danny said, 'Not now, Jack, Mammy Meg and me are talking.'

'You've fallen again, munchkin? Come here for a big cwtch,' she said, arms open, as if welcoming the excuse to change the subject. 'I'll kiss it better.' She looked over at Danny. 'We'll finish this later, okay?'

'No, we won't.'

She looked at him again. 'What's that supposed to mean?'

'I won't be here later.'

'Jack, go to your room babes.'

'I'll be up for a play on your tablet in a bit,' Danny said.

'Listen to Daddy,' Meg said. She kissed Jack's grazed arm. 'He'll be up to put some magic medicine on it.'

Jack stormed out of the room in a teary strop.

'Well?' Meg asked.

'That beep was a text from Sophie,' Danny said.

'Do I want to be hearing this?' Meg said, concern turning to terror in her wide eyes. 'You two aren't—'

'Christ, no,' Danny said. 'I'm taking our two remaining hopes down to the stables at Ely Park, just in case this thing is as catching as we feared. If there's any possibility this bloody thing is airborne, I want the two left standing to stay away until the second lot of tests come back from the lab. I can then put the yard in proper lockdown,' Danny explained. 'That was Sophie okaying it.'

'But … but I've just promised him a room.'

'Well you'll have to un-promise it. I'm sure he'll take it well, charming man that he is.'

She pulled her hair back with a tie. She always did this when anxious, Danny had noticed.

'But I won't feel safe up here alone. Can't you leave the horses where they are?'

'Can't risk it. We need to keep Garrick as a prospective owner. He's a rare breed, more of a philanthropist. Big investors in racehorses need to be mad on horseracing, or just mad. For every hundred quid invested in horseflesh, you can expect on average twenty pounds back, like burning money,' Danny explained. 'I don't want any of this but I'm left with no choice. Garrick's known for lots of things but patience isn't one of them.'

'Why does it always come down to money with you?'

'It's not to buy the latest Jag or Rolex, Meg. I care about money 'cos I love racing. It's the third person in our marriage and I want to stay with it through good times and bad. Right now we only have two owners paying full fees, but the bills keep stacking up, particularly from the vets right now.'

'Couldn't you drop the horses off and come back? Let Sophie take over.'

'They're juveniles, Meg. They've only just settled in here. Imagine what they'll be like moving into another strange place with no familiar faced around to check in on them and feed them, Sophie will be too busy readying the track for tomorrow's meeting. I'll only be away for a few days. None of this is perfect, but desperate times…'

'When you're late coming back from a long roundtrip to the racetrack, I get scared just by the thought of a stranger out there, let alone one already in our home. Danny, please don't go.'

They will come for you.

Perhaps having a strong pair of arms around the place would be a good thing while he was gone, deter and protect against any potential threats out there.

'Gash might be an idiot but he's a harmless idiot.'

'What are you saying now? You want him to stay?'

Danny nodded.

'Jesus, Danny, talk about a one-eighty,' Meg cried. 'Are you just opposing me again for the hell of it?'

'He can help with any heavy work round here until I get back.'

'Is this some mind games, reverse psychology shit? Payback for me inviting him in?'

'I'm just saying he's not a bad person, just done bad things.'

'You were saying he'd rob us blind just now.'

'It'll be fine,' Danny said and kissed her on the lips. 'My mobile is fully charged and I'll leave it on all the time, just in case it gets too much.'

'But—'

'I'm going to load the van up.'

Later that morning Danny was standing by the van, ready to leave. He felt happier Meg had some company.

'Gash, I've indelibly inked the precise level of booze in each and every bottle,' Danny explained.

'Bet your parties are fun.'

'There won't be any parties while I'm away,' Danny warned. 'And be there if we have any other unwanted visitors. Meg is scared.'

44

'You're making *me* scared now,' Gash said, dark eyes narrowing. 'Who the hell are you expecting?'

'Just got spooked by something someone said at Donny.'

'Is that why you said the win was cursed?' Gash asked.

'The deputy head of handicapping reckoned I was in danger. He said *"they would come for me"*.'

'What's that about?'

Danny shrugged.

'You must know,' Gash said.

'Why the hell do you want to know?' Danny asked.

'Whoever it is might think I'm you?'

'We're not exactly twins,' Danny said.

'But they don't know that,' Gash replied. 'What else did the handicapper say? I reckon I'm entitled to know!'

'He was drunk,' Danny said. 'On a jolly.'

Gash gripped Danny's arm until it hurt. 'Tell me!'

Danny tried to shake him off. 'Just look after Meg and try not to be too … you.'

'I need to know,' Gash growled.

'Another word and you'll be on a Bute park bench tonight.'

Danny glanced over at Meg, standing arms-crossed in the black doorway and was thankful she couldn't see Gash's face right now.

'I hope you'll be gone before I come back,' Danny said and turned to climb into the cabin of the van.

He fired up the engine and shifted into gear. He squirmed in the seat when he heard a clattering bang on the side of the van.

'What the hell?!' He looked in the wing mirror and saw Gash's hand on the van. He waved at Danny.

Even when out of sight, Gash still managed to be infuriating.

Danny pulled away.

CHAPTER 6

Danny stared up at the tangerine glow of the pitched roof in his two-berth tent. Without all the daily distractions, the night-time was when all his worries and fears came out to fill the void. He even started fretting whether orange was indeed a positive colour.

Cocooned in a sleeping bag with a night lamp to warm his side, he'd have tossed and turned if there'd been enough room. He checked his watch again. 1.34 AM.

Already, he'd braced the cold to check in on Zebrawood and Pobble Beach housed in the racecourse stables nearby. It was like those bleary-eyed months after Jack and Cerys were both born.

He was about to close his eyes as he didn't want to be completely dead to the world in the morning when he heard a clicking sound outside. He listened intently as the clicks grew louder.

He bolted upright and unzipped the sleeping bag, enough to free both arms.

Danny picked up the night lamp. The tent must've looked like a Chinese lantern in the black of night, he feared. But he felt too vulnerable to flick it off.

He shuffled deeper in, further from the flaps of the tent's mouth. He knew that wouldn't help protect him, like Jack hiding under a duvet scared of the monster under the bed.

Danny unzipped the rest of the sleeping bag and got to his haunches, ready to pounce. He dry swallowed as he watched the zip jerkily part the door flaps.

He quickly grabbed the night lamp as the shape of a head poked inside.

Danny directed the light to splash over the face. He breathed out. 'Sophie? Jesus, thank fuck it's you.'

'Who else would it be?'

'I couldn't work out why anyone would be here unless they were up to no good,' Danny said, putting the lamp down.

'I couldn't sleep, too many things whirring in the mind,' she said, 'and I took a calculated risk you'd be the same.'

He knew there wouldn't be much point inviting her to stay for a while; she was already halfway in.

She shifted the lamp to make some space between them for an Ely Park thermos flask and a tinfoil parcel.

'What were you going to do with that?' she asked. 'Dazzle me?'

'What's in them?'

'Coffee and cookies.'

Sugar and caffeine, Danny thought – just what I need to drop off.

He checked his watch again.

'Relax,' she said. 'I come as a friend not as a boss.'

'People might talk.'

She smiled and then looked around the tent. 'What people? We're alone, Danny, together.'

Danny swallowed again.

'Must say the tent looked bigger from the outside,' she said, turning to get comfy. 'Budge up.'

'I bought it to go camping with Jack on the estate, but turns out he's more into riding ponies than outdoor living, must be in the blood.'

'Never mind, it's probably these legs,' she said. 'Wish I wasn't so gangly.'

'Beats being on the shorter side,' he said. 'Supermodels are revered these days.'

'Shooting up towards six foot didn't make school days any easier, particularly with the surname like Towers,' she said. 'They had a field day, I was Tower of London one morning, Tower Bridge come the afternoon—'

'Towering inferno?' Danny chipped in.

'All right, don't you start,' she said and then laughed. 'I was even called Alton for a whole term. I mean, come on, that's not even tall right?'

'I guess some of the rides are,' Danny said, grinning.

'Whose side are you on?' she replied and play-punched his arm.

She was turning out to be a welcome distraction.

'I remember rushing home from school,' he recalled. 'Getting mam to pencil my height up against the wall, used to stretch every joint and muscle to improve on the last marking.'

'I'd do the same,' she said excitedly, 'except I'd slouch under the pencil. It's funny, we've worked together at meetings for months but I didn't really know a thing about you, bit late now I suppose.'

'And if those shitty classmates saw you now, they'd be as jealous as they ever were.'

'Aww, thanks, Danny,' she said. 'My parents always said I was too influenced by others. I'm enjoying this.'

'Shame it can't last long,' he said, 'I've got to be up first thing, give the horses a stretch.'

'You can virtually do all that on memory,' she said. 'Live a little, have a cookie.'

Danny took one. It's not as if he'd have to make the correct weight anytime soon and the constant stress was burning anything off.

'Look, Danny, the horses are just yards away and you said they'll only need a light canter. You're acting like this is base camp at the foot of Everest.'

'But still—'

'You're hardly being host of the month.'

'But I'm not the host,' Danny reasoned.

'It's your tent,' she said.

'It's your racetrack,' he said. 'Albeit, not for much longer.'

She shifted her weight to look him in the eye. 'What have you heard?'

'That Ely Park was shutting, the land sold for real estate,' Danny said. 'They told me to keep it quiet until the news went public, but don't see any point as you'd have been told ages ago.'

'Who told you?'

'Just some bloke at the BHA,' he said. 'You might have seen him, old guy with crazy hair and glasses, like an old rocker. He dragged me away from Bunce at Donny.'

'I'd heard about the near miss,' she said. 'But I'd left for the parade ring by then. What did this man say?'

'He was just a drunk handicapper,' Danny said. 'Reckoned the future of racing was at risk.'

'That does actually sound as if he was drunk,' Sophie said. 'What made him think that?'

'He didn't say but reckoned he was close to revealing all,' Danny said. 'Even pleaded for me to get in touch if I discovered anything.'

'And have you?'

'Not yet,' Danny said. He pictured the article covering the mystery illness sweeping the country and the only two horses he had left in the stabling nearby. 'Might have to say something soon, it's driving both of us insane at the moment.'

'What do you think he's about to reveal?'

'Perhaps he'll out those behind it all, reveal the truth behind whatever scandal is brewing. Racing needs to clean up its act up right now.' Danny said. 'I still can't believe the BHA approved the sale, there's your scandal in all this – they're supposed to act in racing's interests.'

She moved in closer and with little more than a whisper, said, 'There's a rumour circulating among the clerks of the courses that there's an enemy within the BHA ranks, a rotten apple. His name is Howard Watkins.'

Danny quickly tried to recall if he'd namechecked the handicapper since she'd arrived. 'I never said which one.'

'So it was that same man?'

'Why would the clerks know about Howard?' Danny asked. 'Do you suspect he's linked to the sale of this place?'

'I cannot say.'

Danny was getting the impression Howard's role at the BHA was something far greater than his official job title. 'What name was on the sale contract for this place?'

'Unlike Howard, it seems, I've signed a non-disclosure agreement, and can't give any details until the sale is made public,' she revealed. 'Not even to you.'

'I can't believe the board of directors notified the BHA of their intentions,' Danny said. 'Killing the golden goose, just when you'd turned the track around.'

'Don't set me off,' Sophie said, voice breaking.

'Couldn't you have put your foot down at the meetings?'

'As clerk of the course, I didn't even have a vote, only an advisory role,' she explained. 'Even if I had, it would've made no difference, the vote was unanimous.'

'Who's currently on the board?'

'Powerful people,' she said. 'Heads of business, a surgeon, an MP, even a mayor. They're not in it for the love of the game. If you're thinking of stopping the sale, you're already too late Danny, the deal is done.'

'Couldn't we protest, block the developers at the gate?' Danny said. 'Didn't they campaign to halt Folkestone racetrack being turned into a similar development?'

'I think they voiced concerns that there wasn't enough water to supply an extra twelve thousand houses on the proposed development there,' she said. 'Believe me, I read up on it when I knew this place was under threat.'

'Can't we try the same?'

'Even then, they failed to stop the development and that was Kent, the driest county in the UK,' she said. 'We're in Wales.'

Danny sighed. 'Wait, Hereford reopened after shutting its gates, didn't it?'

'That was only a dispute over lease costs with the council, I think.'

'Anyway, our councillors have been on board for years. Didn't you wonder how easy you managed to make Ely Station a reality?'

'I'd heard.'

'From Howard?'

Danny nodded.

'You must've thought you were helping the track, but the station was just another nail in its coffin. Now any future housing project would have road links to the M4 via the A4323 link road, and a rail network to the rest of south Wales and beyond.'

'Shit.' Danny groaned. 'If I'd known …'

'They've even started the asset stripping here, can you believe it? Everything from the plastic rails to the seats in the grandstand are being sold off at auction, they're even flogging The Whistler statue to melt down for bronze. We just have to suck it up and move on.'

'At least the other racetracks will be beating your door down seeing what you've done here,' Danny said. 'You won't be out of a job for long.'

'They need to have a vacancy first,' she explained. 'There are only fifty-nine clerks in the country right now, one a racetrack.'

50

'Perhaps the BHA will grant a licence for a replacement racecourse in a more rural setting,' Danny said.

'Doubt it,' she said. 'Racetracks must be one of the most land intensive pastimes out there.'

Danny fought back a nervous yawn.

'Let me know if I'm boring you,' she said.

'No, it's not that, it's just, I'd better get my head down at some point.' His eyes felt tired even if his brain didn't.

'I can't leave without taking a selfie,' Sophie said. 'Something to remember this evening by.'

'Okay,' he said.

Sophie was more lonely than she'd let on, he reckoned.

She removed a phone from her jeans pocket. 'Come closer.' Danny leant into the shot. 'Closer still. Jeez, Danny, have you ever taken a selfie before?'

'Yeah,' Danny lied.

He felt the soft skin of her cheek against his.

'Smile,' she said, 'Oh, you've got a bit of chocolate chip on your upper lip. Let me get that for you.'

Before he could react, her full red lips planted a kiss on his mouth. A flood of pleasure and guilt came over him.

Danny pushed her off.

'What?!' she asked.

'Shouldn't it be me asking that!'

'It was a joke. A bit of fun. It didn't mean anything. Christ, Danny.'

'I'm married!'

'Really? It's just you never talk about her.'

'You never asked,' Danny said. 'She means everything. When Sara left me, I never thought I'd find happiness again until I met Meg. She made me feel properly alive again.'

'Have you ever told her this?'

'Some things don't need to be said,' Danny replied. 'I really think you'd better leave.'

'We're still friends,' she said. 'Aren't we?'

'Get out.'

'Are you intimidated by me, Danny?'

'No.'

'Then why are you shaking?'

51

'It's cold.'

'Let me warm you,' she said and leant over to him.

Danny pushed her away again. 'Can't you take a hint?'

'I'll go, I didn't think you'd mind. I thought you liked me,' she said. 'You've ruined a sweet memory.'

'What part of "married man" don't you understand?'

'God, you're old fashioned. Enjoy the coffee and cookies,' she said. 'Choke on them for all I care.'

Flustered, she climbed from the tent.

'Oh, and you promised a big favour in return for staying here,' she said. 'I need a face to meet and greet some VIPs as they arrive by train at Ely platform for our final meeting in the afternoon. Be there at ten-thirty.'

Payback for his reaction just then, he reckoned. Danny had learnt one thing; she didn't take rejection well.

Danny was about to ask if there was any point in showing up when he realised the board members would likely be among them.

'Oh, I'll be there.'

Danny hurriedly leant forward to zip the doors together before she changed her mind about leaving.

What the hell just happened there?

He began to wonder whether he'd overreacted – whether it was indeed just an innocent kiss?

Lying back, he knew his chances of sleep that night had gone from slim to zero.

CHAPTER 7

Danny woke to a buzzing in his ear. His hand came up to swat the insect. As he slowly came around, he realised this wasn't the time of year for wasps or bees. He blinked his eyes open as the buzzing grew louder. Can't be tinnitus, he thought, as it sounded like it was coming from outside.

He sat up, disappointed to be awake yet glad it meant he'd slept at some point. The bright orange glow of the tent told him it was time to work the horses. He crawled forward and stuck his head out.

He looked around but it was like a still photo by the outer wall of the brown-brick Ely Park stables where he'd pitched the tent, close to the hosing down area for the horses. He then looked across to the pitched roof of the grandstand beyond, topped by fluttering Welsh flags.

As he blearily clambered out, he saw the grey dot of a shadow sweep across the tarmac. He looked up at the Wedgwood blue sky.

A drone!

It glided overhead directly for the green of the racetrack.

Must be the TV production crew prepping for the broadcast of the racing that afternoon, he guessed.

He'd read that drones were about to return to help show off the speed and thrills of the race from a very different angle, along with small cameras placed in the stalls and the jockeys' helmets. The aim was to help give the viewer a sense of being in the action rather than a bystander. Drone cameras had previously been shelved after a two-year-old got spooked at the start of a race when they'd been trialled before.

Stripped to his boxers, he had a quick wash down with the hose, all the while anxious another drone might fly over. He towelled down before changing into a fresh, dry sweater and jeans. He shoved his old clothes deep into his kit bag – they stank of Sophie's fragrant perfume. He'd resolved to put them in a separate wash when he got back home.

Turning into the stables to check the horses had a settled night, he saw head lad Jordi stood holding the reins of both the bay

Zebrawood and the chestnut Pobble Beech. He'd already tacked them up and was ready to go.

All the other boxes were empty. Clearly there were no overnighters travelling down the day before among the forty-three runners entered that afternoon, with all set to arrive later in the morning.

Danny hadn't asked Jordi to come down. He pictured the ripped food bag in the barn and the brown paper package at Doncaster.

Was his head lad feeling guilty about something?

He still wanted to see the best in his longest-serving member of staff. Maybe Jordi was just trying to make it up to him for fork-gate.

Not keen to reveal his doubts and suspicions, Danny greeted the head lad with, 'Didn't expect this done for me, it's like having breakfast in bed, this.'

'I drove your car down, I hope you don't mind,' Jordi said.

'No bother, the bus would've taken ages and you're down as the third party on my insurance.'

'Choose your weapon, Mr Rawlings,' Jordi said.

Must've learnt his English watching Bond films, Danny reckoned.

'I'll be on Pobble this time,' he said. 'I'll take us along at a good clip and hopefully this time Zebrawood will assert once we straighten up for the home stretch, understood?'

'Yes, Mr Rawlings.'

'I need to get some confidence back into that one, you see,' Danny said, glancing at Jordi's mount as they walked the asphalt path out on to the racecourse.

They mounted on track and cantered to post round the long sweeping bend into the back straight. Both youngsters seemed relaxed, enjoying the cool breeze and sun on their backs with a surprising hint of warmth for the time of year.

They slowed to a walk at the seven furlongs marker. From there, runners would bank left on the long turn to face the three furlongs of home straight.

Circling at the start, Danny said, 'Mine's a course and distance winner so he knows his way round here. Follow my lead closely and let Zebrawood show his class where it matters.'

54

Jordi nodded.

Danny had never longed to see a rival horse's head draw alongside in a race or workout until now.

'Leave everything out here,' Danny ordered. 'Ready?'

Jordi nodded again.

'Go on lad,' Danny cried and urged Pobble Beach forward. 'Let's set this up for your buddy.'

The chestnut quickly found a good rhythm and took the left turn smoothly on his lead leg.

Making the long bend, Danny kept niggling and kidding him along to ensure there was a proper end-to-end gallop.

Glancing back, he was glad to see Jordi sitting still on Zebrawood tucked in behind. This was more like it.

Reaching the final few strides before they straightened up, Danny was surprised his mount was travelling strongly back on the bridle again. He hoped Zebrawood was too.

Suddenly he felt the colt's legs give way. Before he could feel fear, or anything, he was shunted forward and catapulted from the saddle. It felt like he was tumbling down a flight of stairs having missed a step.

Fired towards the ground, he resisted the urge to shut his eyes.

Instinct made Danny twist in the air. He'd chose a broken collarbone over a fractured skull. He still felt helpless as he could see the impact coming before it happened. This was damage limitation. He wished now he'd packed a back protector.

Almost like a slow-motion replay he could see the grass rising up at him.

He heard a sickening crack as his riding helmet struck the ground.

A whirlpool of light and colour filled his eyes as he flipped over and tumbled across the turf.

When he finally came to rest on his back, the sky kept spinning.

He then heard the thud of hooves and a rush of air as Zebrawood galloped by. His head was banging like the world's worst hangover.

Unlike in a race, there were no ambulances tracking the runners here.

55

Danny was just grateful Jordi and Zebrawood had reacted in time to swerve them. He lay there staring up at the white puffs of clouds, afraid to move.

Soon, the waves of nausea had subsided enough for him to raise an arm. He was almost relieved to feel pain. If there was one thing worse than hurting after a heavy fall, it was feeling nothing at all.

Like most in the weighing room, his worst nightmare was paralysis, to never walk or ride again.

He was glad to see his hand come into view.

He heard Jordi cry, 'Mr Rawlings! Mr Rawlings!'

He then saw a familiar face block some of the light.

'You okay, boss,' Jordi said. 'I get help.'

'I'm fine,' Danny slurred.

'I call for ambulance.'

'I'm fine, really I am,' Danny said. 'I landed on my head, so nothing broke, can't say the same for the track.'

He then tried to laugh, make light of it, but his ribs hurt too much.

'If you want to help,' Danny said and grimaced, 'help me up.'

Jordi ran a hand through his thick black hair. Danny had never seen him so panicked looking. It began to make him nervous.

'I don't want to make it worse.'

'I order you, Jordi, help me up,' Danny said. 'I am your boss.'

Danny raised both arms and was hoisted up.

He held his head to try and stop the trees lining the side of the track from slowly shifting.

At no point did he forget where he was or what had happened. He hadn't been concussed.

'I don't get it,' he croaked. 'One second I was bowling along lovely, the next I had a mouthful of grass.'

Danny groggily looked over at the nearby plastic rails where Jordi had tethered both Pobble Beach and Zebrawood as he'd laid there.

He hoped they wouldn't try to bolt as the interlocking sections of plastic were designed to come apart if charged by a loose horse.

'Are they both okay?' Danny asked. The horses were always his first concern.

Jordi nodded. 'They enjoy the grass, see?'

Danny took a deep breath and then hobbled over to the horses.

He ran a hand down the legs of Pobble Beach to check for cuts or grazes. Aside from a slight mark to the off fore, his ride had escaped unharmed.

'He slid on the ground,' Jordi remarked.

'Unlike me,' Danny sighed feelingly.

'My one is fine too, he's quick at moving to the side.'

Shame he's not as quick going forward, Danny thought. 'Were you about to overtake me when I came down?'

Jordi frowned.

'I'll take that as a "no" then.'

'As you say, Pobble Beach has won here,' Jordi said. 'Mine improves more for the experience here, no?'

Danny couldn't figure out why he came down. The ground was dry, the horse's action had found a nice rhythm and they weren't going flat out turning the corner.

'Was I clear at the time?' Danny asked, checking if they could've clipped heels.

'Yes, Mr Rawlings.'

Danny mood darkened some more. The gallop had underlined Zebrawood's limitations.

He limped back the way to investigate. He skimmed his boot slowly back and forth to sweep the grass like a metal detector, expecting to see a pot hole. But it wasn't long before he came across the opposite, a small mound of loose earth.

Was Ely Park riddled with molehills?

The turf would then be deemed unfit to race, Danny reckoned. He'd seen similar cases force the track to shut for many months.

He followed the path they'd taken on the bend and soon found another. This time there was a clear hoof print embedded in the soil.

Were there other tracks like this? Was this the scandal to end racing?

Danny saw Sophie pacing towards them in a green quilted jacket. She was using her going reader contraption as a walking stick.

It's more than the going she needs to inspect, Danny thought.

He wanted to complain but the look on her face suggested she was about to beat him to it.

'What the bloody hell went on here?' she cried.

'I was about to ask you the same.'

She huffed at the sight of the skid marks on her beautiful turf.

'I'm fine,' Danny replied. 'Thanks for asking.'

'I saw the fall,' she said. 'You shouldn't be out here on a race day.'

'We weren't on the National Hunt track,' Danny replied. 'Your precious jumping ground is still fresh. And we agreed I could work the horses last night, remember?'

Jordi looked at him surprised.

'We both couldn't sleep,' Danny explained, though he knew it would sound worse whatever he'd said.

Fearing a lawsuit against the course or herself, she felt attack was the best form of defence, Danny reckoned.

'Clear the way,' she said. 'I need to check the latest ground conditions for this afternoon's meeting.'

'What's stopping me going to the press about the molehills over there?'

She came storming over. 'I'm surprised you're asking, given you broke in and were trespassing on private land last night, I have CCTV footage as proof. It wouldn't look good for a man with similar previous form.' She pressed the spike end of the stick to his chest.

'You'd invited me,' Danny replied. 'And watch where you put that thing.'

'This *thing* is the Tracktion 2.3 going reader, it's the latest model thank you very much, costs over a grand to replace. And it's a tapered file *not* a spike,' she said. 'You might have helped design this track but thank God we didn't let you care for it.'

Something told Danny she wasn't going to let him off last night easily.

'Jordi, would you take the horses back to the stables?' Danny said. He waited until he was alone with Sophie.

He glanced down at the going reader. The tool had a long spade-like handle, with a box on its shaft, presumably the brains to measure and record all the data. 'Perhaps it should also check if the ground is raceable, not just if it's firm or soft?'

She fixed her gaze on Danny's face as she stabbed the spike into the ground. He looked down. The end had speared the ground just an inch from his riding boot.

'That could've got me.' Danny moved aside. 'You're insane.'

She then pulled back on the handle to forty-five degrees before yanking the end from the ground.

'I'm merely getting a shear reading,' she said. 'The harder it is to pull from the turf the higher the traction and harder the ground. It's supposed to mimic the traction felt by the horse's hoof. It beats sticking in the heel of my welly or the end of a shooting stick as my predecessors did.'

'Just be more careful with your aim,' Danny said.

'You're right, I missed this time,' she said. 'Now do you mind? It already takes me an hour to do a full circuit of the jumps track without having pointless delays like you.'

'Why bother? Just guess, it's your final day,' Danny said. 'Felt like good to firm I reckon, having bounced off it just now.'

'It's mandatory,' she explained. 'Do six measurements at over thirty points on the bloody track. If I don't this final time, it won't look good for my loyalty and reliability when I'm looking for my next job. Without a median going reading figure, I'll be fired before the track shuts.'

Danny had seen the figures in the racecard ranging from zero for heavy as a bog up to fifteen for hard as a road. Most readings were between five and ten. He preferred the old-school going descriptions also still used as a guide.

'Give me your good-to-softs and good-to-firms any day.'

'Well, we both know you're old-fashioned in your ways.' She turned to continue her slow progress round the jumps track, probably hoping Danny would forget about the fall.

'Doubt you'll get much traction in the molehills back there.'

'You can't prove that brought you down.'

'There's one with Pobble Beach's hoof-print in.'

'Well it's a good job we're shutting for good then isn't it,' she snapped. 'Now, let me get on.'

Danny stepped aside.

She seemed more concerned with her job than the fact he'd nearly died out here. He still didn't like ending their relationship like this.

'Oh, and don't forget the meet and greet,' she added, as if to get in a parting shot.

'I'll meet them, can't promise the greet bit,' Danny muttered.

Even from there on the bend, he could see Jordi had already left the racetrack with the horses.

Danny had half an hour before the train pulled in. She'd take twice that time to compile a circuit full of going data.

Plenty of scope for a quick detour via Sophie's office, he reckoned. He wouldn't get a better chance to dig for more details about the party he was about to meet, particularly those behind the purchase of this land.

He didn't feel bad for going behind her back like this; she already thought he was a trespasser.

CHAPTER 8

Danny twisted the handle and was surprised to hear the clunk of a lock turning. He double-checked the brass nameplate on the door to make sure he'd got the right floor. *Sophie Towers – Racing Manger and Clerk of the Course.*

Clearly she'd let security lapse since the news this place was destined for the wrecking ball.

He knocked to check there wasn't a cleaner or removal man in there.

Before entering he glanced at his watch, a habit from his days as a housebreaker when he'd often lose track of time while focused on other things.

Silently, Danny crept into the room.

He felt his pulse quicken. A mix of fear and excitement spiked his veins, like riding in a big TV race.

The long, thin room ran the breadth of the grandstand. He could quickly see why the door hadn't been locked. The room had already been stripped.

The rows of books on racecourse and turf management on the wall had been removed along with the shelves. Clearly the auction was sooner than he'd feared.

The plastic plants and framed photos of Ely races were also gone.

They'd only left a desk with a laptop and on the wall a flat screen showing CCTV shots monitoring various parts of the track.

Danny glanced over at the picture windows each end of the room, one looking out over the paddocks, weighing room and stables to the rear and the other enjoying a panoramic view over the betting rings and racecourse beyond.

On her final-ever going update, Sophie would surely cut corners. He knew he couldn't waste any more time and made for the desk but, as he presumed, each drawer was as empty as the rest of the room.

Even Sophie's leather chair had gone.

Danny hopped on to the desk and rested her laptop on his thighs.

The computer required password entry.

61

Shit!

The only thing in there worth taking was secure.

Danny reckoned he'd only have three attempts. He racked his brains what the password could be.

He typed: *Elypark.*

Password Incorrect. Attempt 2/3.

But then saw a password reminder appear. *A18.*

A18?

Think, Danny think!

She wouldn't have put her age as that would change every year but her birth year would always stay the same.

In the tent last night, he recalled a nickname of hers. He settled upon: Alton89.

PASSWORD INCORRECT. ATTEMPT 3/3.

He knew the laptop would freeze after another failed attempt and she'd then return knowing someone had been there.

He narrowed it down to Alton88 or Alton87.

He thought about leaving but the laptop would still display it was a third attempt next time it was turned on.

Might as well use it up, Danny thought, she couldn't be any angrier with me than she already was.

Without any real conviction, he typed: Alton87.

The screen turned blue. He held his breath.

Welcome flashed up. He breathed out.

As the laptop booted up, he glanced at the CCTV showing Sophie as little more than a dot moving along the backstretch.

On the home screen, he clicked on the file icon named Ely Park Sale and several documents appeared inside.

He went straight to the one named *Sale Contracts* but the heavily redacted documents looked more like crossword puzzles. He could still make out both the purchaser of the land and the planning permissions had apparently been made by the Geneva-based investors under the name of White Turf Group.

Flicking through the documents, it was clear due diligence had been successfully carried out on the consortium, despite them sounding more like a bunch of supremacist gardeners than viable purchasers.

The plans had apparently also faced and defeated various opposition groups and protesters at town planning meetings.

The proposed development had also scored highly in a report on the environmental impact. He could see why as the architects had promised parkland, play areas and even a wildlife reserve.

He opened the development plans. He could see from the key at the bottom of the screen that a doctor's surgery, a supermarket, even a school had been proposed for the land.

His eyes skated over some of the street names on the map. It appeared they were honouring the fallen racetrack by naming the roads after greats that graced both incarnations of the racecourse. Stand outs among them were: The Whistler Way, Golden Fleece Close, Powder Keg Alley.

Powder Keg Alley?!

She deserved more than an alley, Danny thought. Meg will go ballistic.

Why didn't I check any of this more thoroughly before it was too late?

Perhaps he'd become complacent, overconfident that things would never get this far as he was convinced the BHA and Ely board members would never vote to destroy a thriving racetrack. He'd also been so wrapped up with keeping the yard among the winners that maybe he hadn't seen the clues, or perhaps didn't want to see them.

Danny felt hurt that Sophie had clearly kept it secret, though perhaps it was merely to protect him from the truth.

She'd even been trusted with these confidential contracts and plans.

His alert eyes glanced up again. By now she'd made it to the end of the back straight, the farthest point from the stands. From here on, she'd be getting closer.

Closing the file, Danny was drawn to another document in the Ely Park Sale file with the name 'Images'.

He clicked there expected to see idyllic artist impressions of this heavenly utopia but nearly let the laptop slip when he saw the actual gallery of images now filling the screen. They were all still photos of Howard Watkins. In each one, he was wearing the same beige cardigan and purple specs as he had at Doncaster. He didn't appear to be smiling or even looking at the camera in any of them. Danny was pretty confident Howard wasn't even aware these images existed.

Why the hell was Sophie stalking the deputy head of the handicappers?

He started to doubt whether in fact Sophie was there to pick up tips from a top rival track. She must've known by then that the ship she was steering had already sunk.

He clicked on the final image. Despite the blurriness, he could still make out Howard dragging Danny towards the foyer.

Was she acting as Danny's eyes?

She wouldn't be the best witness to the attempted assault; the victim Danny was only in one of these shots and the attacker Jamie Bunce wasn't in any. It seemed Howard Watkins was the star of this show.

Why were they even in this file? Did she suspect Howard was in some way linked to the Ely Park sale?

At Doncaster Howard had predicted the Ely sale and the virus ravaging Silver Belle Stables.

Perhaps he'd get the treble up if horseracing collapsed by springtime, Danny feared.

Howard had urged Danny to come to him if he suspected anything. Perhaps the deputy was protecting himself rather than Danny by stopping any suspicions or accusations reaching higher up in the BHA or the police.

Sweetshop's trainer Bunce had a legitimate motive for attacking Danny following that wayward ride.

Danny recalled Howard was the only regular racegoer to come after him. The handicapper was trembling as he talked about the scuppered gamble. Perhaps it was rage and not fear that was making him shake.

Was Howard the vengeful punter?

None of that could explain why he suspected racing would end.

Danny felt he had to get answers before his yard and the racetrack were both shut down for good.

From his jacket pocket, he removed Howard's calling card. The deputy head of handicapping had wanted him to help. But now it seemed like Danny was the one coming for help.

Suddenly a quiet clicking broke the silence, like he'd heard in the tent last night. To Danny, it sounded more like the ticking of a live bomb about to detonate.

The corridor! The fear was back.

Danny glanced up at the CCTV. The racecourse shots were now empty. He shut the lid of the laptop and returned it to the desk. He then sprinted to the glass wall overlooking the racetrack, a sea of green.

He took a deep, sharp intake of breath to feed his racing heart.

As he heard the door swing open, he didn't immediately turn. He wanted to appear as if he was awaiting her return not dreading it.

'Bet you'll miss this view,' he said unflustered, gazing out while casually placing a hand on the strengthened glass in his best catalogue pose, as if in no rush to leave.

'What the hell are you doing here?' she shouted.

Danny turned to see Sophie resting the soiled Tracktion machine against the wall.

'More importantly, why the hell didn't you lock the door,' Danny said.

'I thought I had,' she said, checking the pockets of her green jacket.

'I didn't leave just in case anyone else came in,' Danny said. 'You were lucky I got here first, so I guarded your stuff.'

'What stuff?' she asked. 'And who else is there?'

Danny glanced at his watch. For the first time, he was glad to be heading for that meet and greet on the Ely platform. Walking by her, he muttered, 'You've changed overnight.'

'Perhaps you never knew me in the first place,' she called after him down the corridor. But Danny's mind was already elsewhere.

He bit back the pain as he limped along the five-furlong tarmacked path running alongside the home straight of the racecourse towards the new train platform that also served Ely village on non-race days.

Beyond the birch trees framing the bend on the far side he could make out the tips of the white speared supports rising up from each corner of the Millennium Stadium off in the hazy distance.

He could easily see why an expanse of flat land within sight of one of Europe's fastest growing capital cities complete with residential planning permission had attracted foreign money in the shape of the White Turf Group.

Danny went the long way round to the station gate rather than hopping over the railings. One fall was enough for today.

Standing on the platform, he looked across at the small station made of Welsh slate and red bricks fired in the new Ely brickworks.

After campaigning to get the station to ferry racegoers here from as far afield as Birmingham, he recalled biting back the tears at the grand opening.

Finding out it was only approved to better the longer-term chances of getting a housing estate project made him want to weep for very different reasons now. Far from breathing new life into the track, this place was its death knell.

The paved platform was plastered with brown and yellow leaves. Not exactly a red carpet, Danny thought, but no more than they deserved.

Looking down the track he could make out the driver's cabin of a train slowly grow larger as it completed the three-mile trip from Cardiff Central.

Lazy bastards could've walked, he thought idly, as the train slowed to a crawl.

Years back he'd have felt nervous, like when prospective owners came to the yard, feeling the need to impress and be liked. But years in the remote countryside, stripped from many of the material distractions of city life, had forced him to face up to his real self and not reflect in the opinion of others.

In any case, he couldn't let Ely Park down as it was already a done deal according to Sophie.

Where the hell were the hacks to ask awkward, probing questions or the protestors with placards and chants?

Danny stepped forward from the gate to direct the suits streaming off the single carriage.

He suspected the party would be made up of BHA bigwigs, councillors, town planners, Ely Park board members and developers. In Danny's mind, he'd treat them the same, all guilty as each other.

He reckoned the White Turf Group would keep a low profile. Investors were normally in it to make a quick buck and then move on to the next deal.

He hadn't expected to recognise any of the arrivals when leading the way he saw Clive Napier step from the train in a suitably funereal black suit and tie.

'What the hell are you doing here?' Danny asked.

'I'm a guest of the BHA.'

Again!? Does he ever do any work?

'Is your deputy in town?' Danny asked.

Clive shook his head. 'We only managed to drag him out to Doncaster as it was the final bash of the season.'

Danny sighed. 'Seems I'll have to go to him then.'

'I'll pass on whatever message you have.'

Danny knew Howard didn't want this to go any higher and Clive would only relay a query or complaint related to a specific handicap mark.

He'd baulk at the questions weighing on Danny's mind, like how could Howard predict the mysterious outbreak of illness in his yard? How did Howard know Danny was in danger after spoiling a gamble in the nursery? And why was Howard's face all over the file linked to the Ely sale on Sophie's laptop?

'I've got a horse that's badly handicapped,' Danny said confidently, as technically it wasn't a lie.

'Give me the details and I'll make sure it gets to him.'

'You know what, I'll leave it.'

Clive's eyes narrowed as if unconvinced by Danny giving up so easily. 'He's a loner. Even if you come knocking, he won't answer you. He wouldn't answer anyone, except perhaps the police.'

'You sure about that?' Danny said. Howard wouldn't have slipped him a card if he hadn't wanted him to call.

'I don't want him disturbed,' Clive said. 'He has far too much work on.'

'Now you're scraping the barrel of excuses,' Danny said. 'You just said Doncaster marked the end of the season for the flat handicappers, they're hardly going to be overworked this time of year.'

'I forbid you,' Clive growled.

It seemed he really didn't want anyone going there. Was he scared Howard would spill some more secrets?

'I don't work for you,' Danny said. 'And how can I ignore a man who predicts the end of British racing? I'm surprised the BHA isn't calling round if I'm honest.'

'It's not the death of racing you should be worried about.'

'Is that a threat?'

'Call it a heads up.'

A deep Welsh voice called out, 'Clive my friend, the free bar awaits us.'

Danny and Clive both looked across.

There was a stocky man, late thirties, short brown hair and clean shaven with dimpled chin and cheeks. He was wearing an immaculate shiny grey suit with a salmon pocket square and neck tie.

'You must be some guy to stop this one getting to the free bar,' the man said, making himself laugh.

Clive smiled politely. 'This is Mayor Reece Porter.'

'Where're your robes and chains?' Danny asked.

'I didn't think it was appropriate on a day like this.'

At last someone could see this was a day for reflection not back-slapping, Danny thought.

'It's a sad day all right,' Reece added. 'But still, like that train over there, when one door shuts another opens.'

'No, it doesn't. All the doors shut and the train pulls away,' Danny said. 'What the hell are you on about?'

'Don't talk to Mayor Porter like that,' Clive said. 'You're the welcome party, what sort of a welcome is this? I'm sorry Reece. He's ambassador and in the circumstances, he's a bit … tetchy.'

'It's okay, Clive, he's passionate about the sport he loves,' Reece said. 'I like that.'

'Well help me, do something.'

'I can't, the time for doing is gone,' Reece said.

'More empty words then,' Danny said.

'I love the sport enough to pay training fees,' Reece said. 'Own a few with Bunce.'

'Jamie Bunce?' Danny asked.

Reece nodded. 'And you think I don't care about Ely Park? I'm a board member here, at least I was.'

The mayor slapped Clive on the back and left with, 'I'll get them in.'

Danny was about to follow Reece when he saw another man approach them.

Danny felt a flicker of recognition.

He had a stern face with cold eyes that could intimidate without even needing to open his mouth. Stubborn strands of red hair valiantly clung to the sides of his bald head, refusing to give up the lost cause. His bushy eyebrows failed to compensate the obvious shortfall in other areas.

Grow them any longer and he could invent the comb-back, Danny mused.

Clive whispered, 'Best behaviour, Danny, it's our chairman, Jacob Rice.'

Danny hobbled forward.

Jacob glanced down at Danny's lame legs. 'It's good to see how inclusive racing has become.'

'I'm not a charity case.'

'He's ambassador, Sir Jacob,' Clive explained.

'Ex-ambassador, after today,' Danny said, 'and soon to be ex-trainer and jockey, but you'd surely know about that, being ruler of the sport.'

No apology came. Danny got the impression Jacob wasn't the type to apologise or feel embarrassment.

Knowing the chairman would soon be needed elsewhere, Danny asked, 'Why did you do it?'

Jacob and Clive looked at each other quizzically.

Danny continued, 'Sign the death warrant for this place.'

'It's for the greater good,' Jacob replied. 'It's best for racing to bury Ely and move on.'

'You're not interested in what's best for racing.'

'You don't know how wrong you are,' Jacob said pointedly and then left for the racecourse path.

'Danny! Are you trying to get me sacked? I told you to be on your best behaviour.'

'That was my best behaviour,' Danny said. 'Why was it good for racing to bury Ely?'

'What?'

'Jacob seemed convinced this place shutting was a good thing.'

'No more questions, Danny. Just give up and go home,' Clive said and shook his head before leaving to catch the others up.

Danny returned to the racecourse car park before he punched someone.

He could only make one link between the sale, the foiled gamble and the end of racing. Howard Watkins.

Danny typed in the Somerset address on the calling card into the GPS of his Honda R8 and revved away.

CHAPTER 9

Danny's knuckles wrapped the green paint of the stained-glass door, louder this time.

He looked across, distracted by twitchy net curtains in the other half of this Edwardian semi. There was a For Sale sign from one of those cheapo do-it-yourself estate agents on their lawn and a Neighbourhood Watch sticker in the window.

Feeling he didn't want to lurk around any longer than necessary, he stepped forward and forced up the brass shutter of the letterbox by fanning two fingers. 'Hello? Howard! It's Danny … Danny Rawlings. We met at Doncaster remember? You wanted me to call you, well, here I am.'

But all that came back were his own echoing words.

He peered inside. Through the depressing gloom, he could make out a red-tiled hallway leading on to what looked like a kitchen out the back. To the right side of the hall there was a staircase facing him. The walls made it seem even darker. It looked tired in there, unloved.

Was he ill? Hibernating? Had he disappeared for a few weeks?

Clive had revealed his deputy would probably only respond to the police.

'I'm with the cops, Howard,' he said. 'If you don't open the door, they will do it for you.'

Suddenly Danny heard the slap of footsteps, then the rattle of a chain and the metallic clunk of a bolt being shot.

When he backed away from the door, the letterbox snapped shut. He didn't want to appear threatening to a man who clearly already felt threatened.

The chain sprang taut as the door opened, enough for Danny to wedge a boot inside. He recognised Howard's purple specs and pallid skin appear in the gap.

'Where are they?' Howard asked.

'I lied, about the cops.'

'I know,' Howard whispered. 'I didn't mean them.'

Danny glanced back over both shoulder. The tree-lined suburban street just outside Taunton was as sleepy as when he'd arrived. 'I'm alone.'

'Why are you here?'

'You told me to come.'

'What do you have for me?'

'Not out here. Let me in and I'll tell you,' Danny said, anything to gain entry.

'Remove your foot,' Howard said.

'And what will you do?'

'Remove your foot!'

Danny knew he didn't want to force the door. The old man looked scared enough as it was.

Howard continued, 'I can't open the door until there's slack in the chain.'

Danny pulled his foot from the gap between the door and its frame.

He heard the clatter of the chain flopping down to hang loose. Howard's face disappeared but the gap in the doorway remained. Danny reckoned this was all the welcome he was ever going to get and pushed the door enough to slip inside.

The thick air was musty in the hallway. Danny was tempted to keep the door open to get some circulation going.

The flight of stairs he'd seen led up to the wall of a landing at the top. He watched for a beat, waiting for a flick of a shadow or creak of a floorboard up there. Nothing.

Howard had vanished again.

'Why did you come?' Danny heard. 'You're making this worse for both of us.'

Danny waved the calling card, unsure whether Howard could see him, wherever he was. 'Like I say, you invited me.'

Suddenly Howard emerged from the kitchen tucking his shirt into the back of his brown slacks. 'I made a mistake, I shouldn't have.'

'Why?'

'We mustn't be seen together,' Howard said, as he stepped into the black mouth of the door halfway down the hall.

'Don't think there's much danger of that,' Danny said, peering into the darkness.

'Come through.'

Cagily Danny followed him in there.

'Your eyes will soon adjust,' Howard explained.

'Do you suffer from migraines or something?'

'I do get them, but usually due to my hereditary light-sensitive eyes,' Howard said. 'Photophobia rules my life.'

'How did you cope at Doncaster?'

'I only came because there was a cloudy forecast,' he replied from somewhere off to Danny's left.

'And your purple specs I guess.'

'You didn't think I was making a fashion statement,' Howard said.

'That's not the only reason you made the effort to go there,' Danny said, 'you knew there would be a huge gamble on Sweetshop in the opener.'

With the faintest of natural light filtering in from the stained glass in the hallway, Danny's pupils grew enough to pick out an outline of the furniture in there.

There was a two-seater opposite a small coffee table and TV. His focus, however, was on a desk against the wall by the door.

He could see the silver lid of a laptop and what looked like a bowl of sweets beside a small desk lamp. 'Before I knock something over, can I switch that on?'

'If you must,' Howard replied. 'Just point it at the wall.'

Danny flicked the switch and could now see a calendar hanging from the wall behind the desk. The sweets in the cranberry bowl were in fact small medals of every shape and colour imaginable.

'War medals?' Danny asked as he fished one out.

'Be careful with them,' Howard snapped. 'They're racecourse badges for annual members. Some are valuable, others are precious to me. Every badge holds significance to me, I choose each for a reason.'

'I'm guessing the designs and colours change for each racetrack with every year,' Danny said, trying to make a connection. No easy task in the gloom. 'You'll soon need a bigger bowl.'

'I only choose one year for each racecourse,' Howard explained. 'I'd already be bankrupt if I collected badges for every course in every year. There have been sixteen hundred racetracks that have come and gone from cities, towns and villages over the past three-and-a-half centuries, from Aintree to York, Aberdare to Yaxley. The names on those badges don't always match the name of the track, like Ely Park is Cardiff's racecourse and before you ask, I neither have a badge for Ely or the original Cardiff races there.' Even from yards away Danny could see Howard's brow had creased, seemingly frustrated by this particular gaps in his collection. 'Yet, after so many have come and gone, there are only sixty left.'

'Fifty-nine after Ely shuts its gates,' Danny corrected.

'I had factored that one in.'

'Are you saying you think there'll be a replacement track, perhaps further out,' Danny said.

'A proposed all-weather track near Newmarket was suggested to help soften the blow of Kempton Park's closure to make way for new housing,' Howard explained. 'I'm sure the BHA will do the same for Ely.'

Danny was heartened by the renewed hope for the Welsh racing scene.

Feeling Howard was opening up, Danny picked a badge out and bent over the desk to be nearer the light. It was circular, aqua blue with gold trim and was attached to a striped cord. He read, 'Berkeley Hunt.'

'How apt,' Howard said.

'I might not be a cockney, but I know enough rhyming slang,' Danny said. 'Are there hunting clubs here as well?'

'No, I think they hold a point-to-point there sometimes,' Howard said. 'I don't know how that badge got in there.'

Danny quickly picked another one out. It was shaped in an elaborate floral design with a red riding cap as its emblem. 'Hurst Park Club 1906. Was that a hunt too?'

'A once-classic racecourse,' he said. 'Yet ultimately doomed, much like Ely Park.'

'Never heard of it.'

'It closed before you were born,' Howard explained. 'Soon after hosting its final meeting on Wednesday 10th October 1962.

One London bookie was said to have laid a wreath round the winning post that day.'

'Why did it shut?'

'Like so many of the others,' Howard said. 'Money. They eventually auctioned off the springy turf to be laid at Ascot, the stand was used at Mansfield Football Club and the railings went to a greyhound circuit apparently.'

'That's where Ely Park is different,' Danny said. 'It makes a profit with all the gate receipts.'

'Wrong,' Howard said firmly.

'It bloody well does … did.'

'I don't deny Ely is profitable. I meant it's not different to Hurst Park,' Howard said. 'It was also popular enough to make a profit at the turnstiles but, as with your local track, not nearly enough to compete with being sold off for valuable Surrey housing stock.'

'So Ely is being shut solely to profit from the land,' Danny said, 'and provide housing.'

'No.'

'Don't talk bullshit,' Danny said. 'I'm no fool, land that close to a capital city will be worth a fortune. It cost Kempton Park, too.'

'I'm not denying those are factors in the sale of Ely Park, but not the deciding one.'

'What is it then?'

'I cannot say, until I share my new findings with Clive Napier.'

'I thought you didn't trust those higher in the BHA. That's why I should come to you.'

'Those in higher ranks,' Howard said. 'Clive is in my department.'

Danny could see Howard wasn't going to share the real reason why the Ely sale had been granted.

'Why are you really here?' Howard asked. 'When it appears you have nothing to offer me.'

'Are my horses being poisoned?' Danny asked, tugging the torn article from *The Racing Life* he'd kept in his jeans.

Howard chuckled.

'You gave me this in the foyer,' Danny said. 'You reckoned I'd pay for getting the favourite beat.' He read the headline out loud: 'Top yards in Newmarket and Lambourn struck down by mystery illness.'

'They are completely unrelated.'

'Really?'

'Really,' Howard confirmed. Danny saw two white discs of reflected light as the old man nodded. 'What on earth made you think an equine illness was linked to a failed gamble?'

'You were talking to my head lad as he slipped a paper parcel into his fleece. Don't deny it, I saw you on the way to the stables where Powder Keg had suddenly been struck down sick.'

'What did you actually see?'

'Jordi putting the parcel in his fleece.'

'Did you see me handing it to him?'

Danny paused. 'Well, no, not exactly.'

'That's because I didn't.'

'What did you ask him to do?'

'Look out for you,' Howard explained. 'Danny, I fear racing's poisoned enough without me wanting to harm the horses.'

'What was in the parcel?' Danny asked.

'Ask Jordi,' Howard said.

Danny didn't know whether to believe his own perceived version of events or that of this stranger.

'Powder Keg must have caught the bug from another horse at Doncaster,' Howard explained. 'Grade One racecourses attract horses from all of the leading trainer centres in that article. And from there, the virulent infection must've spread to the rest of your yard. Even if I was behind this pandemic, racecourses will be forced to shut as a precaution, much like they did for foot and mouth in 2001. No racing means no work for me as a handicapper. You may think me perverse in my ways, but please don't think me an idiot.'

'Then why the hell give me this?' Danny asked, waving the article. 'Along with countless sleepless nights.'

'Turn it over.'

Danny read the article on the other side: *Tributes Pour in as Trainer Larry Wallace Dies.*

Danny still felt bad for forgetting to return the black armband he'd worn over his silks as a tribute riding in the Doncaster nursery. 'You even let me read the other article.'

'I must've been too busy looking for out you in the foyer in case Bunce returned.'

'You rushed down to warn me about this,' Danny said, waving the article.

'That is what I wanted you to see,' Howard said.

'You said I'd put myself in danger after hampering the favourite Sweetshop in the nursery,' Danny said.

'Some months back, certain bookies had raised concerns with my bosses at the BHA about a string of successful gambles.'

'What has this got to do with your department?' Danny asked. 'If there's race fixing by drugging the horses or jockey collusion, that's why the Integrity team are there.'

'They found nothing, no steroids or barbiturates, no suspicious phone activity between the winning connections and punters,' Howard explained. 'Each of the gambles had been at different racetracks and on different going conditions and had yet to use the same trainer or jockey. Even the shrewdest form student or gallop watcher in history couldn't get it right that often. Yet there was no clue or trail as to how they were doing it and the winnings were being syphoned abroad. I felt the only way to find the true identity of those behind these monumental gambles was to find out how they were doing it.'

'What are you? A bookies' rep?' Danny asked sarcastically. 'If a punter can make a fortune from racing, good luck to them, precious few can.'

'No one can be that lucky,' Howard said. 'Only a few out of the several bets got beaten and they were unlucky losers, having been hampered.'

'Sweetshop being one of those unlucky ones,' Danny said.

Howard nodded again.

Danny looked down at the article celebrating the life of Larry Wallace. 'And I'm guessing his horse foiled another of their gambles. He paid for it with his life. That's why you came to warn me.'

'At the time I believed that to be true,' Howard explained. 'The horse he trained, Atomiser, came right across Freya's Folly,

77

who'd been the subject of a biblical flood of money in the hours leading up to a Pontefract handicap. The next day I called him, I told him he was in danger and we arranged to meet at Ludlow. I met him there the next day as he had a runner there, to warn him of a possible reprisal attack.'

'Why did you suspect that?'

'There had been reports of intimidation and abuse on previous occasions when a gamble had lost.'

'That's one bad loser.'

'When I got home from Ludlow races I was shocked but not surprised to hear he had been brutally attacked and left for dead in the red phone box by the betting ring after racing. At the time I'd felt somehow vindicated for going to warn him.'

'What am I going to do?'

'Calm yourself.'

'That's all right for you to say,' Danny replied. 'You didn't knock Sweetshop sideways at Doncaster. It seems like when this bad loser isn't making a killing, he's killing.'

'I've since discovered Larry wasn't killed because his horse hampered Freya's Folly.'

Danny stopped pacing. 'Are you sure?'

'Yes.'

'So I'm in the clear?' Danny said. 'Off the hook for hampering Sweetshop?'

Howard didn't say anything.

'If it wasn't for spoiling a gamble, why was Larry killed?'

'Because I came to talk with him at Ludlow.'

'What?'

'The killer believes I know who they are and the secret behind what they've been up to,' Howard said. 'I was seen talking to Larry, you can fill in the rest.'

'I find that hard to believe.'

'Why not?' Howard asked. 'A minute ago, you believed I was poisoning the horse population.'

'So you coming down to warn me I was in danger is the only reason why I am now in danger and could soon end up full of holes like poor Larry.'

'I feel like the grim reaper.'

Danny started pacing again. 'Why the hell did you come down if you knew I might be butchered next?'

'I didn't know that was the reason at the time,' Howard said. 'You must believe me, I came down in the belief Larry was killed as an act of revenge for costing that "bad loser" a six-figure sum.'

'Hang on, if you know which gambles to look out for, you must know where the gambles are coming from. Why don't you go after them and not just warn the trainers?'

'That is more of an enigma than the method of their selection process. The money flows abroad. The ID of the punter remains mysterious as the method. Clive's insider in the fraud department says the money goes from the betting accounts to an account in Panama to a holding account and the trail eventually ends back in Europe.'

'Doncaster was packed that afternoon,' Danny thought aloud, 'and I was in breeches and vest. Larry's killer would've seen me with you from a mile away— wait, Sophie Towers!'

'What?'

'There were images of you,' Danny said. 'Loads of them, taken at Doncaster that day when you dragged me clear of Bunce on the warpath.'

Dimly backlit by the lamp, Danny's eyes could see from the reflection on the TV screen something shiny between two belt loops at the back of Howard's slacks.

A blade.

He'd assumed Howard had tucked in his checked shirt when it was a knife he'd threaded back there. 'You say Larry was stabbed to death.'

Howard nodded.

'And you were the last person to see him.'

'And?'

'Why would the murderer kill Larry on the off chance you might have revealed a secret?' Danny questioned. 'Surely it would be easier to silence the messenger. You. It doesn't add up.' Danny waited for a reply that never came. 'I think we both know the answer.'

'Well?'

'Well what?'

'What is your secret?' Danny asked. 'The one that Larry paid for with his life.'

'I never told him.'

'So he died for nothing,' Danny said.

Danny saw the blade shimmer as Howard nervily shifted his weight.

'I think I know your secret. It's you that's behind the betting scam. It's you that silenced Larry.'

'Rubbish!'

Howard stepped forward. 'You don't know what you're doing.'

'You're the killer. I can see the murder weapon.'

'I haven't needed this since Larry,' Howard said and pulled the blade from between his belt loops.

'Keep back,' Danny warned, convinced he was facing a killer with a knife in a dark room.

It was now clear why he'd been warned not to come. *But why the hell did he save me from Bunce at Doncaster?* Perhaps this was a personal vendetta.

Danny didn't intend to hang around to find out.

He glanced around for a sharp object but went for the curtains instead. He managed to part them enough to let a heavenly finger of mote-filled light to stream into the room.

Howard fell back, cowering like a vampire.

Danny then ran for the half-light of the hallway. He stumbled, cracking his shin on the corner of a coffee table. He bit his lip as he kept going.

'Don't leave me, Danny,' Howard cried, 'You can't leave. Not like this!'

'Like what? Alive?' Danny snarled as he hobbled out into the hall. He turned and saw Howard surge forward, gripping the knife.

Danny slickly sidestepped out of the way. Howard stumbled and fell forward, head cracking the side of the staircase, as he let slip the blade.

Danny got up and grabbed it.

Howard was now laying perfectly still, head pushed back to a peculiar angle against the panelling under the stairs. In the gloom, he could see blood on the wood where Howard had struck his head though it was harder to distinguish any against the red tiles of the floor.

'Howard? Howard?' he whispered. He was about to shake the body but instinct told him it wouldn't do either of them any good.

He knelt down and check for a pulse. Nothing. He couldn't see his chest moving. Howard was dead.

He fought off the urge to chuck the knife as far away as he could. Instead, he rushed to the kitchen and washed the handle of any prints in the sink as he kept telling himself he hadn't done anything wrong.

There was a struggle. It was an accident. Howard was the one holding the knife.

He reckoned tests would match it to the blade used on Larry. Howard was at the centre of all this.

He was the real killer here!

He was about to call for an ambulance but deep down he knew how all this would look. He was in the house of an old, weak man he barely knew. They'd never believe his side of events, particularly as he'd served time before. He couldn't even say Howard had lunged with the knife without also having to explain why he'd then rinsed the handle.

He had to get out of there. No one knew he was there, not even Meg. If he could get to his car without attracting attention, he could pretend this never happened.

Danny carefully stepped over Howard's body and opened the front door with his sleeve pulled down over his fingers. He waited inside to let his squinting eyes adjust to the bright sunlight outside. He then poked his head out from the door and was relieved to see the road was as still and quiet as when he'd arrived.

He took a deep breath and hobbled from there.

As he glanced back he saw the gap he'd made in the blackout curtains. The nosy neighbours would surely know about Howard's condition. Would they raise the alarm?

Danny glanced across at the net curtains next door. He swore he saw them sway as if they'd just been dropped back into position.

Oh Christ! Danny cleared the small wall at the front of the garden to save touching the gate. He then hobbled to his car safely parked up two roads away.

He felt like hurling up right there but desperately fought off his body's impulse to get rid of the cold service station sandwich he'd forced down on the way there direct from the Ely platform.

His heart was working hard as he accelerated to join the M4 westbound.

Pulling out to overtake a truck, he heard the angry blast of a horn from the middle lane. Danny held up a hand. He was in no state to drive. He kept picturing the net curtains swaying behind the neighbourhood watch sticker.

As he fled the scene, he felt the anxiety growing. Like missing a junction on the motorway, he knew the more he drove the further he was from where he was really meant to be.

Even if he got away with this, he'd struggle to live with himself. He had to admit to at least being there. He couldn't live with the fear of a knock at the door.

Meg would soon pick up on the change in him. A mix of disgust, guilt and confusion screwing with his mind. And he knew the feelings would never go away.

Do the right thing Danny, he thought, as he left the motorway at the next junction and turned back to face his fears.

CHAPTER 10

Danny returned to the now familiar tree-lined suburban road of semis set back by manicured lawns.

As he reached Howard's house, Danny fished for the phone in his jacket. He was ready to call for both the police and ambulance when he saw the curtains in the bay window had been shut again.

Howard was alive!

Danny wasn't religious but right then he felt the need to look up and mouth, 'thank you'.

He'd never thought he'd be so ecstatic to see a pair of curtains drawn. He still needed to be certain. He hobbled up the garden path and spied through the letterbox of the green door.

Inside, there was no sign of Howard's slumped body on the tiled floor by the side of the staircase.

He was about to leave this nightmare behind when he swore he saw the neighbour's net curtains sway again.

More like Big Brother round here, Danny thought, turning the collar up on his brown leather jacket.

Comforted by the fact he hadn't actually witnessed Howard's death, Danny turned to leave with conscience now clear. He still felt bad for Larry. He had to stop Howard before he attacked again.

He looked up at the For Sale sign in the neighbour's lawn and had an idea.

Danny squeezed between two hedges and stepped over the knee-high boundary wall. He then knocked on the red door of the nosy neighbour.

He didn't have to wait long for a man to answer. He was wearing a faded charcoal-grey t-shirt for The Clash's '77 Guns of Brixton Tour. He seemed a bit too old to pull off the wet-look hair and stud earrings. The red Porsche 911 parked outside also screamed midlife crisis.

'Yes?' the man said with a crackly forty-a-day voice.

'Oh, hi there,' Danny said.

'I recognise you.'

Danny edged back. Had he been spotted leaving Howard's house?

'You're that trainer, no, jockey,' the man said, snapping his fingers. 'Wait, Dessie?'

'I'm both,' he replied. 'And it's Danny.'

He didn't know whether to be pleased he had a follower of sorts or disturbed that he could now be placed near the scene of the incident.

He was consoled by the fact that if Howard had killed Larry, he wouldn't be in any rush to report Danny to the police for GBH.

'Derek it is, Del to my mates. I like a bet me, only at the weekends you understand, if the wife's listening,' the man said, tapping his nose. 'She says I'm lucky to have that. What's happened to your place? Not seen one of your runners out for ages.'

'Just a quiet spell,' Danny said. He didn't want news of the illness to get out on social media. Garrick Morris didn't even know. 'I'll be back among the winners soon enough.'

'That's the spirit. Well, give me a call when there's a gamble being lined up,' the man said and then let out a hacking laugh. Danny glanced at his watch. 'Well, well, this is a turn up, what can I do you for Dessie … Danny?'

Danny didn't want to be asking questions about a man he'd left for dead.

He was about to make his excuses when he was suddenly distracted by something over the man's shoulder. At the top of the stairs there was a door. In Howard's house, he recalled there was a just blank wall up there.

Danny quickly changed tack. 'I was thinking of buying a base in the area for Taunton races and saw your sign and thought—'

'Come on in,' Derek said, beaming.

'If it's no bother?'

'It would be an honour,' Derek said. 'Not every day you get a name at the door.'

The man shooed away his curious tabby cat as it brushed Danny's leg.

'Where to start the tour?' the man then asked, flustered. 'Lounge maybe? Sorry, living space the wife told me to call it.'

'What about up there?' Danny asked, pointing to the door on the landing.

'Right you are, boss,' the man said. 'Lead the way.'

Danny pushed the door and entered a small room with an unmade single bed beneath strewn t-shirts and shorts, and Liverpool Football Club squad posters were pinned to the wall.

'Excuse the mess,' Derek said. 'It's my youngest, he's yet to understand the concept of clothes hangers.'

'No matter,' Danny replied distantly, as he knocked the wall dividing the two semis. He could hear a hollow echo, which made no sense. There was no door to a room the other side. He put an ear to the wall but heard nothing.

'The walls are thick,' Derek said. 'They don't make them like this anymore.'

'Are the two semis a mirror image of each other?'

Derek nodded. 'Both hallways run down the middle, so you won't become experts in the neighbours TV tastes, not that you'll have any trouble with Howard. The model neighbour. He's in the racing game too, a handicapper, I think.'

Danny asked, 'Does he ever talk shop?'

'He doesn't talk much about anything,' Derek replied. 'I would say pop round and introduce yourself, but I suspect he doesn't appreciate visitors.'

'Why?'

'He doesn't get any,' Derek explained. 'He barely gets out, my missus worries about him, I tell her to leave him be, he seems happy enough for—' He stopped, as if feeling it wasn't for him to talk. 'Any case, he's not in right now.'

Danny swallowed. 'Really?'

'I heard the door slam shut.'

'When was that?'

'Why are you here, Danny?' Derek quizzed.

'To check out your house,' Danny reassured.

'It's just … you seem more interested in next door.'

Danny didn't want Derek getting any more suspicious. He was surprised he'd opened up this much for him. The house had clearly been on the market a while.

'Look, I'll go away and think about it.'

'Don't you want to see the other bedrooms,' he asked though it came out more like a plea. 'You haven't even asked how much it's on for.'

'Go on.'

'Three forty.'

Surely the high-roller Howard could've afforded a detached property or at least do up the one he'd got next door, Danny thought. He guessed there wouldn't be much point as he was the only one who saw the place and it was mostly shrouded in darkness anyway.

'The master bedroom's just at the end there if you'd like to—'

'You know what,' Danny replied, 'I'm not looking to go over three hundred.'

'I'm open to offers.'

'Let me go away and think about it,' Danny said, before leaving abruptly.

Along the garden path, Danny looked back to see Derek had stayed watching him right to the gate. He was glad to see the red door finally shut.

When he felt a cold gust of wind take his breath, he heard a distant thud of a door.

Danny looked back to see if Derek had reappeared, but it had come from Howard's door which was swinging on its hinges. Derek wasn't kidding when he'd said the door had been slammed.

He knew Derek probably wouldn't have had time to get to the bay window of his lounge to spy on him.

Seeing no one else around, Danny saw an opportunity. From the pavement, he leapt back over the front wall. He bit back the pain as he rushed to the open door before those net curtains twitched again. He stepped inside, soon swallowed up by gloom.

Danny knew Howard was in no state to go far, most likely concussed from the bang to his head at the very least.

He checked his watch: eleven fifty-two and twenty-three seconds … twenty-four.

He'd seen nothing in the lounge that might reveal the Howard's secret. He looked up to the wall at the top of the stairs where he'd seen a room next door.

Climbing the stairs, he could see the wall appeared to be at an angle, like some optical illusion. At the top, he worked out that the wall had come away and was swinging loose, like the front door.

As he suspected, a false wall. He knew whatever he was hiding behind there was worth losing the residual value of a bedroom upstairs.

Softly, Danny called for Howard but was met by silence.

He pulled the false wall open enough to peer inside. There was a room about the same size as the kid's bedroom he'd knocked on the other side of the wall to his right.

He could see a desk, filing cabinet and empty shelves. He set about searching the place; it didn't take long. Like Sophie's office, it had already been cleared.

Had Howard panicked, taking incriminating evidence behind the gambles with him?

Danny shoulders dropped slightly. He was about to leave when he felt something stick to his Nike trainer. He peeled away what looked like a postcard from the grip of his sole. He flicked on the single bulb behind a dark shade.

It appeared to be a colour image, an aerial shot of a racetrack.

Having helped design both the flat and national hunt tracks, Danny instantly recognised the left-handed track with easy bends. Ely Park.

There was a clock on the image. It had been taken at eight thirty-four that morning.

That was about the time when I'd been woken by the buzzing, he recalled. The drone!

Why had Howard commissioned a drone to take stills of Ely Park?

Was it to check for more molehills? Perhaps he reckoned it wasn't deemed raceable.

Danny scratched his head. The more he knew the less he seemed to know. It became clear the owner of the house he was in remained a mystery.

At first he couldn't decipher the image as it appeared to be covered in dirt. Perhaps the floor was in need of a clean like much of this house.

He tried to wipe the grime away on his t-shirt but it kept snagging on the material. He rubbed a finger over the photo and felt it was sticky. He held it closer to the dim light of the shaded bulb and could make out a red footprint. He looked down. There was a trail of blood on the floor.

Danny felt his nostrils to check for a stress nosebleed he used to get as a kid. His fingertips were clean. He crouched and touched the sticky blood stains.

Howard had indeed been up here after the tumble, Danny reckoned.

Having learnt from his mix up with the newspaper cutting, Danny turned the photo over. On the back, he saw two columns of numbers – each to one decimal place and ranging from five point one up to nine point seven.

It reminded Danny of sectional times where the race was dissected into the time taken to complete each furlong to give punters a better idea of the pace at different stages. It was regarded as an important tool in the punters' armoury and was commonplace in Australia, the US and parts of Europe, but had taken longer to be introduced to British racing. But he was quick to rule that out, as it took over ten seconds to complete each furlong, even in a top-class sprint at a sharp track.

Beside the numbers he also noticed someone, presumably Howard, had sketched two concentric semicircular arcs like a rainbow or maybe a horseshoe.

Acutely aware he wasn't meant to be in the house, particularly in this bit, Danny didn't have time to give the scribblings much thought. He just slipped the photo in his combats and did a quick shuffle to wipe any remaining blood on to the carpet, leaving messy red skid marks rather than identifiable footprints in case Howard or the police saw them.

Danny crept down the stairs. He was about to leave the way he came, sensing he'd already pushed his luck, when he heard a faint noise.

Treading softly along the hallway the noise grew louder, a soft metronomic tap every few seconds. It was coming from the black of the front room.

Danny's heart quickened some more. Every instinct told him to run while he could but he wasn't going to leave without checking the BHA laptop in the lounge. He went to the kitchen. On the wooden sideboard he was relieved to see a blade that looked like the one he'd left there.

Danny picked it up and returned to the lounge. He wanted to be better equipped for the rematch if Howard was back in there.

Entering, he flicked the light on.

He froze as his wide eyes tried to take in the scene. Howard's body lay hunched over the desk bathed in a lake of his own blood, arms outstretched and wiry hair now sopping and dyed crimson red. A steady waterfall of blood trickled over the edge tapping the stripped floorboards.

This time, Danny was left in no doubt, Howard was dead.

Danny's free hand went to his mouth. This can't be happening!

He knew head wounds bled more. But was the impact from stumbling head on into the staircase that bad?

Should've caught him, he cringed, not stepped aside.

He also wished he'd never returned. He knew the horror of witnessing this would stay with him, like a scar, faded by time but always there.

Danny studied the streaks of blood up the wall forming the Roman numerals XII. He made out the red enamel badge embossed with Middlesex County Racing Club.

Why did Howard waste his precious final moments to select that badge from the bowl and then protected it under his fingers?

Danny looked up at the spattered wall calendar with today's entry left blank.

Must've struggled back here but then realised there was no phone to call for help.

This was his final message to the world.

Time to leave!

He returned to the hallway and then stepped out into the blinking sunlight, heart pounding even faster than when he'd last left there.

He'd only got halfway down the front path when he heard footsteps from behind.

He ducked in between bushes separating the two gardens and crouched low seeking cover.

From down there he saw enough to catch a glimpse of the other visitor's legs as they walked by. He saw tan leather shoes with gold buckles.

'Howard's dead,' a man's voice remarked angrily.

Danny made himself as small as he could.

As soon as the sound of slapping leather on tarmac had gone, Danny felt it safe to emerge. He got to his feet and left before anything else could go wrong.

CHAPTER 11

Keen to avoid all the number plate recognition cameras on bridges over the motorways and toll booths at the Severn crossing, Danny drove north to join the Heads of the Valleys road linking up the top ends of the South Wales valleys.

As he snaked the A road, he didn't take in any of the rivers, valleys and thick forests either side. His mind's eye could only see blood, all over the desk and the floorboards and up the wall. XII.

Danny pulled into a truckers' lay-by and searched online for the significance of the number twelve. Among the results that came back were the signs of the zodiac, the sons of chief Norse god Odin, the days of Christmas, the month December, the members of a jury and the apostles.

But would Howard honestly waste his dying moments leaving cryptic clues? Would he really act like an oddball to the very last?

Made no sense, Danny thought, surely this was about something closer to home. Something he was passionate about. He seemed all-consumed by the betting scam and the sale of Ely Park.

Danny recalled Clive saying there were thirteen handicappers, including himself. Perhaps Howard sensed he was about to die and then there would be twelve. But why bother to tell the world that? And the fact he'd written the numerals Roman-style must itself have meaning.

With his prints and DNA likely to have been left somewhere at the scene, Danny needed an alibi and fresh clothing.

He couldn't put this on Meg. She had enough to deal with mothering two kids and twenty-seven mostly sick horses.

And while old pal Stony would always be willing to help, he couldn't be trusted to get the story straight. His memory wasn't as reliable as his character.

He struggled to think of anyone else he could trust. Then, he recalled the handicapper Alex Park he'd met at Doncaster lived in Penarth, nearby.

Would he be in? Would he even let Danny in? Why should he?

Not keen to switch his mobile on right now, he called upon the laptop he always kept in the boot as a back-up. Searching the BT directory online he found the address of the handicapper.

He hit the steering wheel. At the very minimum he was guilty of leaving an injured man for dead. He'd struggle to convince himself he'd acted in self-defence against a weak old man, let alone a jury of strangers.

Why the hell did I reach for that knife?!

He now realised he'd also washed away Howard's prints from the handle. Saying he'd been attacked with that knife, Danny would then also have to admit to tampering with evidence.

He parked up in a visitor car park in Penarth, a village overlooking Cardiff Bay basin from the west.

Although close to breaking, he couldn't let it show. The story of Howard's death wouldn't break for hours if not days or weeks, given his lack of visitors.

He limped by lifeless yachts with clinking masts moored up on the rippling black waters of the marina.

From there he could see the white Norwegian church on the other side of Cardiff Bay and the ring of slowly revolving red dots on the Big Wheel by a bustling hub of bars and restaurants.

He glanced further off to the shimmery copper of the Millennium Centre's shell, apparently host to classical concerts, plays and operas. It had never been Danny's scene but he was open to change. He felt ready to take Meg to see a show as he'd promised time and again, perhaps have a meal out, like normal couples seem to do. He wanted to feel that; a more stable life and relationship that training racehorses could never provide. Right now normality felt a lot more distant than across the water there.

The job was always going to consume their lives but it appeared the endless hours of sweat and tears had finally ground them both down. And for what, a string full of sick horses who'd even struggle to win races when well, for a yard dependent on a local track about to close.

For the first time since taking out a trainer's licence, disillusionment had got a grip. His love for the horses and the competitive spirit to make it work could only stretch his resolve so far. He now felt a responsibility in finding a more steady income to support two hungry kids.

Perhaps his mam would finally see her son get the 'proper' job she always longed for. She still hoped to see him in a smart suit and immaculate haircut carrying a shiny briefcase.

Meg had warned him to just dip a toe into the water with the flat horses, not quickly wade in neck deep.

As he limped on desperately searching for the help of a comparative stranger, all of those work worries had been sent to the back of a long queue.

He zipped up his brown leather jacket to hide the smear of blood from wiping the photo on his t-shirt.

He had to be strong to keep a clear head if he was to get out of this mess.

He soon arrived the address for Alex he'd found online. He peered beyond the black railings of the security gate to a modern development of three-storey link-detached houses in honey-coloured bricks with white window frames and garage doors. It felt dead, soulless. Danny reckoned Ely Park would be like this in a few years.

On the intercom, he pressed button nineteen. He opened his mouth when a buzzer sounded and the gates glided apart.

Head down and jacket collar up, Danny bit back the pain as he headed for house number nineteen on the corner.

Alex was already standing in the door with tea towel slung over his shoulder. 'Please, come in out of the damned cold. This is a surprise, what brings you this way?'

He was just glad of the warm welcome. In his current state, he could've cried from such a small act of kindness.

'Are you alone?' Alex asked, closing the door with a rush of cold air.

'Yeah,' Danny said as he walked into an open-plan living area with whitewashed walls, laminate floor and a cream leather settee with chairs.

'Come through, I've got some pasta bubbling away if you're peckish,' Alex said, 'always put too much in the pot.'

Danny felt sick. He wanted to reveal all, unburden his soul, but knew he couldn't.

'You've missed a cracker of a tennis match,' Alex said. 'It's the final set now but there was a forty-two shot rally in the opener. Are you a fan of other sports?'

'What?' Danny asked, mind still working out how he could play this.

'Tennis,' Alex said. 'I'm mad on all sports really, you name it I'll watch it.'

'Don't really get the time.'

Alex smiled. 'I guess as a handicapper I've got it easy compared to you trainers.'

'You're telling me,' Danny replied and forced the semblance of a smile.

'Well?'

'What?' Danny asked, panicked as if he'd done something abnormal.

'Why the surprise visit?'

Danny didn't have an answer. He could hardly tell the truth. That he'd left Alex's colleague to die alone.

Yet he needed a change of clothes and an alibi once that truth came out.

Alex broke the awkward silence with, 'Doesn't matter, shouldn't have asked, you don't need an excuse to call round. Take your jacket off, make yourself at home,' Alex said. 'I'll hang it up.'

Please don't be nice, Danny thought, make this any harder.

Danny never felt comfortable expressing himself with words, probably why he bonded better with horses. But he suspected not even words would get him out of this.

He peeled his jacket off.

Alex held his hand out but didn't grab the jacket being offered. He appeared to be distracted by Danny's t-shirt.

Danny looked down to see a red skid mark across his chest where he'd wiped the sticky photo.

Alex frowned. 'What's that?'

Good question, Danny thought. He had to think of something in a few seconds or it would smack of a lie whatever came out.

'Well?'

Suddenly he had an idea. 'It's lipstick, I'm having an affair. I tried washing it off but it's like a permanent marker that stuff.'

Alex laughed. 'Bloody hell, Danny, always thought you might be a dark horse.'

Danny felt lying about an affair was better than the truth.

'What's her name?' Alex asked. 'She a looker? Must be if you're playing away when you've got that lovely wife of yours at home. You should use her more as a rider, got talent that one.'

'I can't say,' Danny said playing coy, though right then he'd have struggled to even make up a name. 'I reckon I've already said too much.'

'I hear ya,' Alex said, running a pinched finger and thumb along his lips. 'Flattered that you thought of me as your confidant.'

'I'm here for more than a confessional.'

'Go on.'

Danny looked down again at the grey t-shirt.

'You'll find clean clothes in the spare room second door on the landing, you've got the pick hanging up on the left.'

'Cheers,' Danny said and sighed. 'I'll give you them back.'

'Nah,' Alex said. 'You saved me a trip to the charity shop.'

'I'll be sure to make a donation,' Danny said.

There was a pause before Alex said, 'What are you waiting for?' He motioned with his hands to the staircase.

'There's something else Alex,' Danny said. 'I need you to lie for me.'

'Lie for you?'

'Yeah, if Meg asks why I was out this morning, I need you to say I was with you.'

'Why would Meg ask?'

'If she suspected something, I'd tell her I was here this morning. If she, or anyone for that matter—' Danny said, stopping short of mentioning the police. 'Just make sure my story stands up, I was with you this morning, all morning. Watching that tennis match if you like.'

'Um, okay,' Alex said. 'Not particularly happy about that, but—'

'I'll make a bigger donation,' Danny called back as he thudded up the stairs before Alex changed his mind.

In the spare room, he picked out a black t-shirt and stonewashed denims plus a pair of moccasins.

From up there he could see out the back. There was a metal dustbin in the middle of the paved back patio. He looked closer

95

and saw it was an incinerator He'd use one similar for household waste back at the yard.

On the small square patch of lawn he saw a pile of branches and twigs.

He looked down at the incriminating t-shirt and combats held at arm's reach, safely away from Alex's clean castoffs.

He came back down. Alex was stirring his pasta.

He carefully handed Alex the clothes. Danny then nervously watched as Alex inspected the t-shirt and then placed it on the tiled area by the island in the kitchen off the lounge.

Wordlessly Alex went over and picked up the phone on a side table by the settee. 'Find out about what, Danny?'

'The affair.'

'There is no affair,' Alex said.

Danny tried to shrug off the cynicism with another nervy smile and shake of the head which felt more like a twitch.

'Why would I lie about an affair Alex?' Danny reasoned. 'Risk wrecking my marriage.'

'That's not lipstick on your t-shirt. That's blood,' Alex said. 'Now can you start telling the truth?'

'I cut myself.'

'Cut yourself? Why not get a plaster like the rest of us?' Alex said.

'No, I remember now, it was a nosebleed. Had them since I was a child.'

'Since when do you need an alibi for a nosebleed? Now, start telling the truth!'

Danny felt like he was about to reveal a lifelong secret that had been left to eat away at him. He hoped the telling would be the worst part.

'Howard is dead.'

'What?!' Alex asked.

'Howard Watkins, the handicapper, is dead.'

He thought sharing the secret might help ease the pressure. It didn't.

Alex ran a hand over his short hair. He now looked as bad as Danny felt.

But Danny couldn't quit and leave now, he'd already said too much.

'I said the truth, Danny.'

'I swear,' Danny replied. 'Why would I lie about something like that?'

'When?'

'This morning.'

'This morning?!' Alex replied, frowning. 'Why hasn't Clive rung me?'

'He doesn't know, no one knows apart from me … and now you.'

Alex muted the TV and turned to BBC news channel. 'Can't think straight, don't need distractions.'

Fearing his mug shot filling the screen, Danny found the news channel more distracting than some tennis match.

'This makes no sense,' Alex said. 'Are you saying you discovered him?'

Danny's silence spoke volumes.

Alex glanced back at the t-shirt and combats on the kitchen floor. 'That blood, it's not yours is it.'

'He came at me, with a knife,' Danny explained, palms up.

'Holy fuck, you … you didn't, please say you didn't,' Alex said. His hand rubbed his scalp harder this time. 'I'll be implicated. Harbouring a murderer, isn't that what they call—'

'You invited me in.'

'I thought you were here to ask about the handicap marks of horses in your yard, not to confess a murder.'

'It was an accident, I never killed anyone.'

'Why have you come here then?'

'You were my last hope, I couldn't risk telling the ones I love.'

'Last straw, more like,' Alex said. 'Wait, you were after an alibi to the murder.'

'My DNA is at the scene.'

'And so should you be, answering police questions.'

'They won't believe me,' Danny said. 'But there's a chance you will.'

'Why? You lied about the lipstick,' Alex fumed, and then grabbed the handset from the table. He began to dial a number.

'What are you doing?' Danny asked.

'What you should've bloody done in Taunton.'

'Put the phone down!'

Danny saw a knife on a wet chopping block on the kitchen island. He picked up the razor-sharp steel blade. 'Believe me, I don't want to be doing this but I don't trust you.'

'Believe me, the feeling is mutual,' Alex replied. 'Handy with a knife are you?'

'I never touched him,' Danny replied.

'Look, Danny, we both know this isn't you,' Alex said, brown eyes widening. 'Put it down.'

'Not until you put that down,' Danny replied.

There was a standoff until Alex slowly rested the handset back on the stripped wood of the coffee table.

As Danny came forward, Alex backed away.

Danny picked up the phone and on the display he could see Alex had already punched in the second nine. He cleared the screen and slipped it in his pocket.

'I want you to leave,' Alex said.

'Is that an incinerator out the back?'

'No way,' Alex said. 'You're not destroying evidence in my back yard. I won't have it.'

Danny was already reaching under the sink for a small canister of lighter fluid. 'It'll get rid of the clothes, not just the stain, just in case I was spotted leaving Howard's place. Better chance I get off, the less likely you'll be implicated.'

'It's a windy day,' Alex said. 'It'll send smoke signals to the neighbours and half of Penarth that I'm harbouring a murderer.'

'I'm not a murderer,' Danny said, waving the blade. 'Anyway, you've got a pile of branches out there, perfect excuse for a fire.'

Alex grimaced.

'Now go,' Danny ordered, waving the knife.'

'First put in the t-shirt and combats, then some twigs and add a splash of this,' Danny said, glancing at the canister he'd just put on the granite top.

Alex went for the kitchen drawer under the sink.

Danny lunged forward, grabbed his arm and put the blade to his throat.

'You're hurting me!'

98

'I'll hurt you more if you do something like that again,' Danny said.

'Matches,' Alex replied. 'I was getting matches, that stuff won't light itself, for good reason.'

Danny eased off.

Through the kitchen window, he watched as Alex dropped the clothes by the rear wall.

'What the hell is he doing?' he muttered.

Was he going to make a break for it over the nearest fence?

Danny rushed to the kitchen door but then saw Alex had now gone over to the incinerator and turned full circle. He then looked in the bin.

'Come on Alex, be a good boy now.'

He then came back and returned to the incinerator this time with the soiled clothes.

He followed Danny's orders.

A trail of smoke soon began to rise up into the clear sky.

Alex came back in rubbing some life back into his hands.

'Why did you turn round?' Danny asked. 'Were you looking out for a neighbour.'

'Yes,' Alex replied. 'But not to rescue me. I needed to know I wasn't being watched.'

'Were you?'

'Would I have come back with the clothes if I was?'

'You didn't put some of that wood on,' Danny said.

'There was already some in there,' Alex said. 'Anyway, this isn't Guy Fawkes night, we don't want an inferno and then believe me, the neighbours will be watching. Let the lighter fluid do its job.'

Danny returned the knife and made for the front door.

'What makes you think I won't go straight to Penarth police station with this?' Alex asked.

'I'll just say you knowingly aided a criminal.'

'You wouldn't.'

'Like you said, I've already lied to you, about the blood on my t-shirt, lying to the police won't be any harder,' Danny said, 'and the security cameras above the gates will show I was here for quite some time. It'll be your word against mine.'

'Get out,' Alex said. 'And don't get flashed by the speed cameras on your way back. Pretend this never happened.'

'But if it hits the fan and I'm called in,' Danny said, 'we've got each other's back, right?'

Alex paused too long.

'Don't overthink this, Alex. Remember, I can drag you into this,' Danny said. 'Being my alibi will be a whole lot easier than being my accomplice.'

Alex gave the faintest of nods.

'Let's hope it doesn't get that far, for both our sakes,' Danny said. 'I don't take any joy from this, but I will drag you down if I need to.'

He left quietly.

As he reached the perimeter gate, he made sure the cameras captured his best side.

Back at the car park, he flicked on his phone to tell Meg he was coming home when he saw there were eleven missed calls and four voicemail messages. He presumed they were from impatient owners nagging for updates but all the calls were from a single phone number, Meg's mobile.

Danny checked his watch. 3.22 PM.

She knew he was due to meet the welcoming party at Ely station and must've realised that it might drag on with a free bar. He had expected a few calls having kept his phone off since leaving the meet and greet but to get eleven in the space of just a few hours made him nervous.

Had the police come knocking already?

Dusk was taking hold as Danny crept up the shale driveway of Silver Belle Stables in his Honda.

The light was on their master bedroom at the front of the trainer's cottage. He could make out Meg's shapely shadow pacing back and forth across the drawn curtains.

Danny was relieved there were no squad cars waiting for him. He hoped the DNA tests from Howard's house would take several days to get back.

He still braced himself for a stern questioning inside.

CHAPTER 12

The night light above the front porch of the trainer's cottage flashed on in a blaze of white as he parked up. He noticed a flickering yellow glow through the downstairs curtains. He couldn't wait to get inside to feel the warmth of that crackling log fire and smell the wood smoke.

Upstairs, he could see Meg pacing lengths of their bedroom. Cerys must be teething again.

He turned the key in the studded oak door.

As he stepped into the blackness of the hallway, Danny sensed the atmosphere in there was as cold as outside.

On the rare times he'd return early from a day at the races, Danny would normally be met by a wave of unconditional love welcoming him home, putting the day's misery into perspective. But right now, when he needed that most, it wasn't there.

Jack would normally race into the hall skidding on the Welsh slate out of excited anticipation, followed shortly by a beaming Meg holding a sleepy Cerys in her pink Babygro and a bottle of baby formula.

There was an eerie stillness now. The sweet smell of bubble bath had drifted from upstairs.

As he opened the lounge door opposite a large Welsh dresser in the hall, he was about to ask Gash to go check on the horses, give Danny and Meg some rare alone time.

But it was Stony who was sat upright in the maroon leather chair near the hearth. His white hair and pink face were glowing in the roaring fire. He cradled an empty tumbler on his thigh.

Danny was drawn to the toasty warmth of the hearth. 'Stony? Wasn't expecting you here.'

'Neither was I,' Stony replied glumly.

'See you've found the drinks cabinet.'

'Meg said to help myself.'

'I'll go check on her,' Danny said.

'No!' Stony ordered, waving a hand. 'Don't, not yet.'

'Why?' Danny replied with a perplexed smile.

Stony just nervily scratched his white hair and checked his watch.

101

'Stony, what's wrong? You're worrying me now.'

'She'll come down in her own time, when she's ready.'

'If you're not going to tell me, I'll just ask her.'

Stony got up and beat Danny's lame legs to block the door.

'What's happened, Stony? This is killing me,' Danny said. 'Wait, where's Gash?'

'Gone.'

'Really?' Danny asked, just to be sure. 'That's the first bit of good news I've heard all day.'

Stony suddenly shivered.

'You can't be cold with that thing going by your side,' Danny said, dazzled by the licking flames.

'I was just thinking of Gash,' Stony said.

'Why did he leave?' Danny asked. 'He had it made up here. I was expecting to have to chuck him out.'

'Come sit down with me,' Stony said. 'I'll get you a stiff one. I'm afraid it's not good news.'

'Okay,' Danny said slowly. 'Average news will do.'

Stony didn't reply.

'Stony?'

Stony just went to the drinks cabinet and poured Danny a worryingly large measure of single malt whisky.

'Where's Jack and Cerys?' Danny asked. 'It's too early for bedtime.'

'Jack's playing in his room, I think Cerys is sleeping up there bless her.'

Danny put his drink down. 'Sod this, I'm going up.'

'She won't thank you for it,' Stony said. 'And I don't want you overreacting, doing something you might regret.'

'Jesus, Stony,' Danny fumed and then downed the two fingers.

'It's not as bad as you're imagining,' Stony said, 'but it could've been.' Stony then added in a whisper, 'And reading between the lines, I think she partly blames you.'

'For what?' Danny asked. 'How can I be blamed for something I didn't know has happened?'

'Just wait a while, let her explain.'

'What exactly did she say?'

102

'Let me see, she went … if that bleep Danny comes back and bleeping tries to come up the bleeping stairs, you have my permission to punch his bleeping lights out,' Stony recalled. 'Like I said, I'm only reading between the lines.'

The pair sat silently listening to the distant creak of floorboards above.

Stony kept sipping away, eyes looking everywhere but Danny. The air felt thick with the atmosphere of a dentist's waiting room. Danny had never seen Stony this sad with a free drink in his hand.

'How did you get here? You don't drive.'

'Taxi, I ran up the drive. Think I need a sports bra.'

'I wouldn't.'

'I know, I know, I don't do sport.'

Danny asked, 'Do you know what the significance of the number twelve has with racing?'

'Twelve?'

'Yeah, XII.'

Stony stroked the white bristly stubble on his chin. He never normally left his house without shaving. Clearly Meg had asked him here in a rush.

'Backed a twelve-to-one winner the other day, took the price,' Stony said. 'It's s.p. was only tens, mind, so don't know whether that counts.'

'Doesn't matter,' Danny said. He hadn't expected anything so wasn't disappointed. He knelt by the fire and warmed his hands.

'What about the year 1966 or the Middlesex County Racing Club?'

'It's not quiz night, Danny.'

'Think,' Danny said, face tickled by the heat.

'1966? England's World Cup win? Can't think of anything special to do with racing,' Stony said. 'The only track in Middlesex is Kempton Park.'

'Hmm, that's all I got, too,' Danny replied.

'Have you checked the internet, lad?'

Danny nodded. 'Other than Middlesex County Cricket Club, not a lot else I could find there.'

'No surprise,' Stony said. 'A lot of Middlesex has been gobbled up by London's suburbs in recent decades, much like Kempton will be I'm guessing. What is it – an owners' club?'

'An annual member's badge,' Danny replied.

'Bit odd they went for that mouthful, Middlesex County Racing Club, when Kempton would do.'

'Apparently many of the badges didn't have the name of the actual place on the badge, like Cardiff's racetrack is ... was known as Ely Park races.'

'Was?' Stony asked.

Danny had forgotten the news of Ely shutting had yet to go public. 'Ignore me, I've had better days.'

'Never mind, lad,' Stony said. From his cardigan pocket, he pulled a blank green and white betting slip, with matching pen, nabbed from his local bookie The Flutter House.

'Middlesex County Racing Club,' he muttered as he scribbled it down.

'Can't have been as bad as mine,' he said. 'You've heard The Flutter House has moved out of the city centre. Got to walk an extra half mile there and back. Blamed it on a big pay-out.'

'Was it you?'

'I'd be getting a stretched limo there if I had.'

'If you think of something about that badge, give us a bell,' Danny asked.

'Is it important?'

'Don't know yet.'

'Leave it with me,' Stony said. 'My brain doesn't work so quick no more.'

'Cheers, Stony.'

'Still, it's not all bad news.'

'Why?'

'At least the BHA has softened the Kempton blow by possibly adding an all-weather track someplace, they reckon around Newmarket, makes sense over the cold winter months, I guess, seeing there's over a hundred yards there and horse population of three thousand I'd read in *The Racing Life*,' Stony said, 'perhaps they've got a replacement track for Ely Park when it goes, further out from the city like. They do say when one door shuts another—'

'Opens,' Danny interjected. He put his drink down. 'That's just what the mayor said, on Ely platform.'

'Always fancied myself as a dignitary,' Stony said.

Danny recalled Howard chose every badge for a reason.

Had the Middlesex badge been picked out for a reason as he bled to death? Given the parallels with Kempton, was this badge Howard's best way of trying to link his attacker to a planned replacement track for Ely?

At least now Danny felt there might yet be hope for racing in the area, albeit further out from the city. 'Thanks, Stony.'

'Don't know what for, but I'll take it.'

When a funereal thud of heavy feet could be heard coming down the stairs, both of them looked over at the lounge door.

'This is where I leave you,' Stony said and rocked himself up from the armchair. 'Good luck, mate.'

Danny swallowed. It was the not knowing.

'Shall I book a taxi?'

'Already done,' Stony replied. 'When I saw your headlights come up the drive.'

Meg came in.

Even from there, Danny could see her eyes were pink.

Wordlessly she hugged Stony, who then quietly let himself out.

'What has Gash done?' Danny asked, fearing the answer.

'Nothing,' she said sombrely and blew her nose.

'What's this about then?'

'He did nothing only 'cos I managed to fight him off,' she said.

Danny felt the tension ease.

He watched as Meg tugged her hair tie loose and then pulled her blonde hair back into a ponytail – her inevitable tell for when she was stressed, like whenever Powder Keg ran.

'Are you sure nothing happened? You're not protecting me from hearing something I don't want to hear?'

'Believe me, the way I felt about you when your phone kept going to voicemail, I would let you know.'

Danny went to put an arm round her. She shrugged it off.

'No, Danny, not yet,' she said. 'I'm not even close to forgiving you.'

105

'You said nothing happened,' Danny said. 'And even if it did, why is it my fault?'

'You left me up here by myself with that monster,' she said. 'What part of that isn't your fault?'

'Well, it won't happen again.'

'Of course it will happen again,' she cried. 'You see, the lab tests results have come back.'

Danny pictured the squad cars with flashing blue lights speeding along the country lanes towards the yard. His heart leapt as if a charged defibrillator had been pressed to his chest. 'What?'

'The blood tests,' she said. 'The horses are on the mend. A few even ate up this morning, and all appear to be over the worst.'

Howard was right; the illness wasn't linked to the betting scam or the Ely sale. He needed to speak with Jordi, apologise for treating him so coldly in recent weeks. He couldn't believe now that he could even have suspected his head lad of treachery, poisoning the horses he was supposed to care for. Stress of a yard in lockdown had messed with his mind.

'But that's great news!'

'It also means that our yard will start having runners again soon and that means it will happen again, you leaving me up here on my own fending for two kids alone in the dark,' she said. 'Don't make promises you can't keep, Danny.'

'I'll delegate, promote Jordi to travelling head lad,' Danny said. 'Don't be like this, Meg – you're normally the bright, bubbly one here. Leave the cynicism and grumbling to me.'

She took his whisky and downed it. 'I feel like getting drunk out of my frigging mind.'

'Are you ready to tell us what happened last night?'

'Nothing happened, all right?'

'So why are you like this?'

'I'm effed off right now because he put me in a position where it could have happened. I don't like feeling helpless, vulnerable,' she explained. 'Up here all alone with that ... if I hadn't kick him in his ... brains, both of them, I might've been a lot more upset right now.'

'How did he make his move?'

She sighed and then chewed her lip. 'He showed me his—'

'Jesus, he didn't,' Danny quickly interrupted her. 'I don't think I want to hear this.'

She continued, 'He showed me his betting account.'

Danny pictured the heavy losses in the account Gash had shown him when pleading poverty and asking for a room for the night.

'He was trying to impress his way into my knickers.'

'Really?' Danny asked. 'What was his record?'

'Trust you to ask about the betting first.'

'Was he losing?'

'No,' she said. 'I only spotted two losers from the several bets on the screen, Sweetshop and Freya's Folly.'

'Then what?'

'As I looked at the screen I felt a warm hand slide up my thigh,' she said. 'That's when I threw a punch, his phone went flying. As he scrambled for it, I kicked him where it hurts. And if you're at all bothered, he kept his wandering hands to himself after that and left soon after. I locked the windows and the doors just to be sure, even kept the fire on just in case he tried the chimney, though the fat creep probably would've got wedged.'

'Did you call the police?' Danny asked.

'Do you think I should?' she asked.

'I'd leave it,' he said, trying to act cool, as if he hadn't fled a crime scene hours earlier. 'I think you did the right thing.'

'Why didn't you just say there was no free room in the first place?' she asked.

'He said he'd changed,' Danny explained. 'He didn't say for the worse. And he's clearly got at least two accounts,' Danny said, excitedly. 'He used his losing personal account to get pity from me and another winning account to get you. Gash must have a new high-roller punter as a new client. Are you sure Freya's Folly and Sweetshop were the only horses that lost?'

'Yes,' she said. 'Only 'cos he told me to ignore them as they were "unlucky losers".'

Danny recalled Freya's Folly was hampered by Larry Wallace's horse Atomiser and Sweetshop had been interfered when Danny cut across for the gap near the rail at Doncaster.

Meg continued, 'He said "Here's my chance to be with a winner for once". His breath was warm and wet and it stank. What the hell did you see in him as a friend?'

'I didn't,' Danny said. 'He was a middle man between me and a betting syndicate, placing bets recommended by me with their pooled money and transferring the winnings back to them. It seems from that betting account he's still in the game albeit for a different high roller. He'd better watch his step mind, I'm starting to think this client is a bad loser.'

'Why did he say he was skint?'

'I don't know,' Danny said. He began to wonder why he'd really turned up unannounced after all those years. 'But I do know that I'm proud of you. He's some lump to fend off.'

'Swear it's my Welsh-Italian genes that helped,' she said. 'Joe Calzaghe and Enzo Maccarinelli got nothing on me.'

'You've rarely talked about your Italian nana since our wedding day.'

'I like to keep her in here,' she said, pressing her hand against her chest. 'I get upset otherwise, she was the one that got me into dancing. She came over from Bardi and helped set up an ice cream parlour with my Welsh bampi. She'd settled quickly there as she reckoned the Welsh and Italians were similar in always putting family first above all else.'

'Does that mean we're good?'

'We'll never be good while you're barely here,' she said. 'You know Jack asked for jockey's silks for Christmas – he wanted to be like daddy.'

'That's good,' Danny enthused, 'the boy's showing ambition, focus even at that age.'

'Not because he necessarily wanted to be a jockey,' she said 'He'd seen more of you riding on the racing channel than he did at home; he thought they were your normal clothes.' She looked down at the baggy t-shirt and ripped stonewashed jeans. 'Mind that's probably a good thing. Seriously, are they a cry for help?'

'I'll bin them,' Danny said, secretly glad of an excuse to put Alex's castoffs in with the other rubbish. The fewer reminders of the day the better. 'I'll give up anything to get back *us*.'

'What about this place?'

108

'Bloody hell, Meg, that's a bit of a leap in sacrifices, from Bros jeans to the whole estate.'

'Well?'

Danny could see this was some kind of test to prove his love and loyalty to her. 'If it meant you were happy.'

'I just don't think I can get to spring with no adults to talk to most evenings. It makes me feel vulnerable, lonely, scared, I'm doubting myself more and more. I couldn't even face going into Cardiff for Christmas shopping, the crowds made me anxious. I used to be confident when I sometimes met my old Rhymney girlfriends. They've noticed a change in me, too.'

'But you always said you were independent.'

'Independent, not a bloody hermit.'

'What about Kegsy?'

'We'd find a small caring yard and I'd go visit regularly. She'd get even more attention there than she does here.'

'You're asking me to give up a lot, racing's always going to be a massive part of my life, it's part of me,' Danny replied.

'I know that, all I'm saying is … all I'm saying, we're not going to look back at the end of our lives wishing we'd spent more time saddling up a gelding for a selling hurdle at a rainy Towcester, even if it happens to win.'

'Nothing wrong with a seller at Towcester, a win's a win.'

'That's not my point and you know it,' she replied. 'We'll be cwtching up, remembering the times we had together, us four maybe more, that's what'll make our hearts sing.'

'This is all very lovely but it won't pay the bills until we get to retire.'

'I know,' she said, 'but there's such a thing as a work–life balance.'

Danny wondered if it was *her* crying for help. He put a hand on her thigh which was promptly removed.

'No, Danny, I need some space.'

Danny got up and walked to the door.

'Where you going?' she asked.

'Give you space.'

'You're just running from your problems again.'

'Well, I won't be running far,' Danny said. 'I'll be in my office just up there at the end of the landing where all the work happens.'

Meg hit back with, 'You'll find a duvet and pillows in the airing cupboard where I leave all the laundry, that's also at the end of the landing.'

Danny would normally go to the spare room after a falling out but they'd recently converted that into a nursery for Cerys. Now it seems he was demoted to the office, though it would've been easier to sleep in an actual dog house than on that stiff chair designed more for supporting a straight back to keep him awake and alert for work.

He spent a few hours staring at the wall, lost in worries.

Howard seemed convinced Larry had been silenced because they'd met up at Ludlow.

Danny recalled Howard wouldn't reveal a thing without talking to Clive Napier first. His boss also appeared to be his confidant.

Danny now felt bad for swiping the badge from Howard's lifeless hand, perhaps inadvertently blocking a private message between Howard and Clive.

Danny had to warn the head of the handicappers he might be in danger and pass on the enamel badge.

He sat up, not particularly keen on adding his neck to the list of his aching muscles.

As the clock ticked high up on the wall, he became increasingly aware that he hadn't heard Meg retire to the master bedroom. Night-time paranoia made him worry Gash might come back for a second try.

He crept along the landing checking in on Jack and Cerys, jealous they could sleep so deeply. He guessed they didn't have a worry in the world. It made him feel like adulthood was overrated. He silently negotiated the stairs.

In the orange light of the dying embers of the lounge hearth, Danny could make out the shape of Meg curled up on the sofa, tumbler on its side on the woodblock floor.

Danny returned to the airing cupboard and softly spread a sheet over her. As he stood there staring down at her perfectly still, delicate face her blue eyes suddenly opened wide. Danny didn't know who was spooked the most.

'Bloody hell, Danny,' she croaked, sitting up. 'You scared the life out of me. What time is it?'

'Late,' Danny whispered as he gently balanced himself on the edge of the settee. 'You must've passed out after a few drops of the good stuff.'

Danny stroked her blonde curls.

'Were you staring at me asleep,' she said, propping a cushion behind her back and then rubbing her eyes.

'It's just, every time I look at you, I'm shocked.'

'You charmer, you.'

'No, I'm shocked you ever went out with me let alone marry me. I used to watch you marking out your dances on your own 'cos you didn't want bruised toenails from my two left feet.'

'Bet you thought I was proper mental, then,' she said, smiling eyes sparkling. 'If anything, dancing helped keep madness away, helped take my mind off a bad racing result or one of Jack's tantrums.' Meg shut her eyes. 'I remember, like it was yesterday, sat on my nana's knee, she'd whisper, "watching you dance made my heart dance".' Her smile disappeared. 'I wish she was around. It makes me sad she never got to see my successes on the dancefloor and racetrack, and what we'd built up here, together, the two of us,' she said. 'How do you cope with your dad missing the best years?'

Danny paused. 'I reckon ... our closest family and friends always see the best in us about everything, right?' She nodded. 'Even though your nana only saw you starting out as dancer and rider, I can guarantee she'd have already have imagined your successes. Chances are everything she'd imagined and dreamt for you was even better than the real thing, apart from your future husband, of course.'

She stifled a laugh. 'The other day I found myself searching online for classmates that made my life hell at school,' she said. 'I hoped they'd failed in life, particularly that bitch Elly Williams. Does that make me a bad human?'

'It just makes you a human,' Danny said.

'Have you ever searched out the kids that made your life a misery?'

'Would be quicker to tour the prisons,' Danny said. 'Look, deep down, everyone wants to see themselves doing well but using your ex-classmates as a gauge is pointless. Stony always tells me, "life ain't a race" and he should know, he's watched enough of them. Everyone's rushing about trying to desperately achieve something or find happiness, and I guess I'm guilty as the rest. I think above it all, you're making me learn what's really important and it all comes back to family. I think I'd have liked your nana.'

'She'd have liked you,' she said and then got up.

'You can come back into *our* bed if you like,' she said, stroking his forearm with a finger.

Danny wanted nothing more, but he needed to get away at first light without being noticed. He owed it to Howard at least. 'I'll stick to the office just for tonight, love. I know I won't sleep now and I've got some invoices to sort through.'

'I wasn't thinking of sleeping,' she said, biting her lip.

Danny moved his arm away. 'I've been bad, I need to be punished.'

'Um, that's a bit kinky but I'll try.'

'No,' Danny said. 'I mean I need to pay for the way I've been, make me feel better I suppose. You don't mind?'

Her face dropped slightly.

'Suit yourself, your loss,' she said and left, sheet trailing behind her like a comfort blanket.

Danny returned to the racing office at the end of the landing.

Staring up at the office ceiling, he had resolved to leave before first light. He felt bad for breaking a promise not to leave Meg alone he'd made just hours earlier but he had to do this.

Clive Napier wasn't expecting him. Danny reckoned that was a good thing. He doubted Clive would've accepted an appointment anyway and a surprise visit would mean no time to rehearse answers.

CHAPTER 13

'Why are you here, Danny?' Clive asked, glancing both ways down the corridor before shutting the door behind them.

'You invited me in.'

'You refused to leave the corridor if I didn't,' Clive replied. 'And even then, you invite *yourself* in!'

Danny was already seated in the fourth-floor office lit by windows looking down on High Holborn in the heart of the city. Sophie's office had more soul and that was empty, Danny thought. It reminded him at least he didn't have a desk job.

The potted plants looked fake and the industrial grey filing cabinets matched the carpet.

The only valuables Danny could see in there were Clive's sharp navy suit and the gilded frame surrounding a portrait of the BHA Chairman Sir Jacob Rice on the wall behind Clive's desk. The artist had clearly been told to go easy on the bushy red eyebrows and saggy jowls.

'Guess I was wrong,' Danny said, looking up at the picture.

'About what?'

'He *is* an oil painting,' Danny said.

Clive smirked. Danny was surprised by the apparent lack of respect he held for his boss.

'You don't think he's up to the job, then?'

'The BHA has kept this sport better regulated and freer of corruption than any other country,' Clive said.

'You say that in the past tense. I'm guessing you think this current chief isn't fit to run it.'

'No comment.'

'I'd have flipped that round by now then.'

'I'd rather keep my job,' Clive said, 'and I don't seem to have a problem with authority, unlike you.'

He dropped on the padded swivel chair. On the desk, Danny had spotted today's copy of *The Racing Life*, a laptop, BMW key fob and a mobile. 'He sometimes does the rounds, checking in on the licensing, media and HR departments before us.'

'I'd been to the disciplinary department enough as a jockey but didn't know there were so many others.'

'Well, now you do,' Clive said flippantly, glancing up at the wall clock. 'How the hell did you even get past reception?' Danny didn't immediately reply. 'You know what? I don't think I want to know. Skip straight to why you're here.'

'Isn't it obvious?' Danny said. 'Howard's dead.'

'Do you think I need this right now?'

'That's probably what Howard would've said,' Danny replied. 'If he wasn't lying dead in a mortuary.'

'It's my wife's birthday,' he said, frowning. He picked up his phone and the background wallpaper of the screen showed a smiling glamorously dressed brunette in a hugging white blouse with a glass of champagne on a sunny day with what looked like the rolling Sussex Downs as a backdrop, probably Glamorous Goodwood.

'You look upset,' Danny said. 'Have you forgotten to get a present or something? I'm sure she'll cope and there are more important things that need sorting.'

Clive glared at Danny.

'All I'm saying, make it up to her next year,' Danny added, but the look on Clive's face suggested it hadn't helped.

'This is your last chance before I have you arrested for breaking and entering. Why the bloody hell are you here?'

'I want to know if Howard got to share his secret with you before he … you know.'

'Why are you so interested?'

'He told me I was in danger,' he said. 'That I might end up like Larry if I'd been seen talking with him at Doncaster.'

Clive tapped the table and eventually broke the silence. 'I wouldn't have said this as I know Howard wanted this kept secret, we both did, but that seems less important now in the circumstances. He cleared his throat as if about to make a speech. 'Howard was agonisingly close to a breakthrough in solving Case Twelve when out of the blue the integrity department shut it down.'

'Case Twelve?' He pictured the bloody streaks forming XII up the wall behind Howard's desk.

'The integrity department have to deal with several investigations on the go to help ensure the continued smooth running of the sport.'

'I didn't know. What kind of cases?'

'Where there's money to be made in any walk of life, criminality is never far behind. We need to root out the evil corrupting the sport before it grows. Every successful investigation is a deterrent to ward off future ones. All this goes on silently behind the scenes, with many unsolved cases never seeing the light of day,' Clive said. 'That way there's no panic or loss of confidence between punters and the sport.'

'What was so special about Case Twelve?' Danny asked.

'It appeared unsolvable,' Clive said. 'The winning punter seemed to have the Midas touch but the integrity department couldn't work out why. Either they were from the future and had brought with them the results pages, or they had insider knowledge that no one else could possibly have, which is the best kind. If you and you alone know a result before the race, you'll get the best odds all for yourself.'

'Perhaps that was why it was shut, the rulers of the sport here didn't want it rocked by scandal,' Danny said. 'How did the BHA justify closing it publicly?'

'They didn't need to as it never went public,' Clive replied. 'Privately the chiefs blamed a drop in funds due to a fall in bookies gross profits made from racing after some big pay outs to this gambler and a drop in betting turnover as punters start turning their back on racing after these puzzling gambles. A double whammy for the levy fund.'

'And to fund prize money,' Danny said. 'Which would put trainers like me out of business in no time.'

'If it was left to rot we couldn't afford to govern the sport, let alone fund it. For whatever his reasons, Sir Jacob's decision to close that case to save funds would cost us all infinitely more in the long term.'

'Why the hell did they close it then?'

'My insider in the integrity department reckoned it was on orders from upon high. Short term damage limitation, taking the politician's line of "kick it into the tall grass", I think his exact words were. Really it was to let future chairmen deal with Case

115

Twelve on their watch when it finally comes out long after Rice switches blazers and retires to his gentleman's club.'

'Kick it into the tall grass,' Danny whispered. On the Ely platform, he'd heard Jacob say something similar about the racetrack. 'Bury Ely Park.'

Howard was convinced the sale and scam were linked, Danny recalled. It seemed like that was yet another moment of clarity. He'd been right about everything else.

Jacob Rice clearly wanted both the Ely sale and the scam covered up. He could see why a scam might be damaging to confidence in sport but why would the sale of a racetrack?

Danny was haunted by the red graffiti again. 'Why did Howard refer to Case Twelve as XII?'

Clive leant forward, casting a shadow over the desk. 'Where the hell did you hear that from?'

'Don't panic, it was Howard,' Danny replied, 'the only other working on the case. He told me at Doncaster.' Danny resorted to the half-truth as he wasn't particularly keen to place himself at a scene where he'd left Clive's deputy for dead, a hit and run of sorts.

Clive's eyes fixed firmly on Danny. 'You see XII *is* the case. When it was officially shut, I went against protocol and unofficially kept it open, instructing our best numbers man, Howard, to keep researching possible theories as to how the punter was consistently picking winners. He was more than willing. We weren't going to allow this to fester with the betting coups growing in size and regularity as the punter grew richer, cockier and greedier, until the damage to the sport's reputation had become irreparable. For one thing, as head of the handicappers I would be made the scapegoat for not detecting the problem earlier. I knew using the words Case Twelve in update emails between us would be picked up on internal security filters here, so we decided from then on to use XII when discussing details of the case.'

'What had Howard just discovered that the killer didn't want us to know?' Danny asked.

'We'll never know now. Howard has taken his secret to the grave.'

'I wouldn't be so sure,' Danny said. 'Howard was determined to share his findings, probably fearful he'd put himself in the firing line, the XII he'd shown me was to say his death would be linked to Case Twelve. Only you were aware of this. This was a message directed at you, Clive. He wanted you to know his death was because of the case he was investigating.'

'I knew he shouldn't have come to Doncaster,' Clive said. 'He'd normally turn the invitation down due to his hatred of light and other people. But this time we'd convinced him to come, seeing as it was the final meeting.'

'Howard also told me your insider at the integrity department found nothing except all the gambled winners were in handicaps.'

Clive nodded.

'Inexplicably it seems the punter somehow knows which horses are seriously underrated in handicaps and are therefore carrying much less weight than the horses ability deserves,' Clive explained. 'There are a growing number of races going into the form book that aren't all they seem.'

'Are the horses assessed by different handicappers?'

'Yes, and cross checked,' Clive said. 'To the naked eye, the handicap marks are one hundred per cent accurate, based on previous form achieved on track and the overall age and profile of the horse.'

'Like fake news, racing has fake form,' Danny said.

'Except fake news can be separated from real news with research,' Howard said. 'This fake form appeared impossible to decipher from real. Every race was televised and the collateral form was there for all to see in the formbook, except seemingly only one person on this planet knew which were rigged in their favour, the mysterious gambler. All the numbers were in order, but the horses were easily outperforming them without the need to pump them with steroids.'

Danny paused. 'Perhaps Rice up there was right, let it pass and move on as it's only one punter.'

'While the amount of fake form in comparison to the overall form book might seem like just a piss in a swimming pool, would you climb into that pool?'

Danny shook his head.

'The form book is the punters' bible – it's how most pick out their selection. If they find out that it's riddled with lies they will soon walk away from racing and put their money on so many other sports. Racing's levy is now directly taken from bookie profits, taken from bets on racing. If this is ignored, where's the deterrent for others thinking of doing it? And without handicap races the sport would die. They make up sixty per cent of the races in the fixture list and as they are the most popular type of race for punters due to their competitiveness, they yield an even higher proportion of the betting turnover. Manipulating form will undermine punter confidence as they won't know the real from the fake. Without authenticity and integrity handicaps will die.'

'I can now see why you two went behind his back,' Danny said, glancing up at the oil painting.

'Howard was right, racing will collapse if we can't find how they are beating the handicapping system; the same one that has served us so well since Admiral Henry John Rous perfected with weight-for-age allowances. And once certain form is devalued or overvalued, those horses will continue to race against each other and collateral form will then become distorted too. With one punter creaming off all these millions and losing punters refusing to lose to a seemingly unfair rating system, bookies profits and therefore levy will be squeezed from both ends. I remind you this place is funded by the levy, it won't just be Case Twelve that's shut down the longer the scam continues.'

'Howard seemed convinced that the Ely sale and the punter were in some way linked,' Danny said.

'There's no pattern,' Clive said, as he typed something into the laptop between them. He turned the screen to face Danny. Not one of the bets was at Ely there were races all over the county. There doesn't seem to be any pattern to work out how they have fooled both punters and handicappers.'

'Not all the handicappers,' Danny replied. 'Howard wasn't fooled.'

Danny stared at the screen. He quickly recognised it was an online betting account. He was proud to have resisted the urge to bet for years but he still knew the intricacies of the art of punting. The bookie Bestie Bets had clearly taken a drubbing with a long list of winners. In fact he could only see two losers among them – Sweetshop at Doncaster and Freya's Folly at Pontefract, both costing the punter five grand. The same losers Meg had spotted when Gash was bragging.

'Minimise the screen,' Clive said.

'I haven't finished looking yet,' Danny said as he scanned down the screen, photographic memory soaking up every detail.

'That doesn't matter, just do it.'

Danny clicked the underscore in the top right of the screen to reveal another screengrab was open beneath, different bookie this time but identical list of bets.

Danny clicked to minimise and revealed another hugely successful online account on the page. And again.

'These were all opened by the same person. I did well to get these hacks before the accounts were closed by the bookies.'

'Gash Rahm?'

Clive knitted his fingers together as he sat back in his chair. 'You're good.'

Gash really was in on it, Danny thought, and he'd let him stay at the yard.

'I can't believe I was so gullible,' Danny said. 'Good for nothing, slimy shit-face sex fiend.'

'Don't beat yourself up.'

'I wasn't.' Danny gave him a look. 'He turned up at my place, out of the blue asking for a room.'

'Make him leave. His intentions aren't good.'

'You got that right,' Danny said. 'He made a play on my wife but didn't even know I'd remarried when he arrived.'

'You knew him before?'

'Years back,' Danny said. 'But that's a time I'd rather forget. Howard did warn me they would come for me. I didn't bank on it being that corrupt piece of shit.'

Clive said, 'When the BHA checked him out, he came back as clean as the horses he was backing.'

'He's a born loser.'

'He can't be the main man then,' Clive said. 'The gambler at the centre of this knows what they are doing.'

'Oh, I know for a fact he's not the mastermind. He's a placer of bets for bigger punters that struggle to get bets on with bookies as they close their accounts or limit stakes. Perennial winners aren't good for business – only losers like Gash are

119

allowed to get lumpy bets on with bookies,' Danny said. 'It looks like they stung the bookies for the best part of a million quid in all these accounts.'

'And the rest,' Clive said. 'He's milked them till it hurt, all the big bookies and even your local The Flutter House in Cardiff got stung for seventy large.'

Explains why they had to move to smaller premises out of the city centre, Danny thought, recalling Stony moaning about the walk.

'How did you know Gash?'

'He's an ex-colleague,' Danny said. 'I'd pass the bets on for him to place on behalf of rich clients in and around London mostly.'

'Well, make sure he's gone.'

'He already has,' Danny said. 'Meg saw to that.'

'He came for what you had learnt from Howard.'

Danny recalled Gash's almost feverish interest in Howard as they stood by the van waiting to rehouse Pobble Beach and Zebrawood for a few days at Ely racetrack. 'Do you really think Gash could've killed Larry and Howard?'

Clive nodded.

Danny didn't think Gash had it in him, but then again he didn't think he could be a sexual predator. 'You never really know the whole person I guess.'

'I know mug punters well enough, I used to be one. They haven't got the skill, discipline, patience or shrewdness to consistently get the kind of results in those accounts,' Danny said. 'No, I'm the last person to defend Gash, but he's working for someone and taking a cut, he's not the murderer.'

'You've been wrong about him before.'

Clive seemed keen to pin the blame on someone.

Bit too keen, Danny thought. 'Anyway, Gash was still at my yard when Howard was stabbed.'

'He is a lucky boy.'

'Howard told me the winnings are wired offshore some place exotic, but where exactly does it end up?'

'If the money had air miles, they'd be even richer,' Clive said. 'It went from Panama to a holding account in Holland, trying to lose the scent of any future investigations if we can prove any wrongdoing on the race fixing side, but my insider believes the money finally settled in Geneva.'

'Geneva?'

Clive nodded.

Danny recalled the contract he'd found on Sophie's computer, more specifically the purchaser of the Ely Park land, the White Turf Group, was based in Geneva, Switzerland. Howard was right again.

'It's the White Turf Group,' Danny said. 'They are the link between the Ely sale and the betting scam. They were buying the land using the betting profits probably as a down payment. That's why Jacob Rice wanted the sale to bury Ely and the scam to be kicked into the tall grass.'

'You're very good,' Clive conceded. 'But client confidentiality makes it extremely hard for us to put individual names and faces to a group of investors in a private account based abroad unless we have enough to prove serious fraud has taken place at the racetrack. We have nothing. There is nothing in the handicap marks or form of the horses bet in those accounts to suggest otherwise. We have nothing on them. I should've closed Case Twelve and then Howard would still be alive.'

'But we have the betting accounts. Gash's high roller has to be up to no good, no one is that lucky.'

'All those accounts show is a successful gambler, not a fraudster. They're a winning punter, a rare breed. Any bitterness would come across as jealousy. Let's face it they're the one that got away with murder, quite literally.'

'We might not have concrete proof but at least we now know the White Turf Group are investing their dodgy winnings in prime real estate,' Danny said.

'A million pounds is only going to buy a few acres of land with planning permission in sight of Cardiff, this isn't Austin Powers, Danny. Remember, the White Turf Group is a consortium of investors of which this punter is merely one, albeit they are clearly as persuasive as they are manipulative, convincing other rich players to get on board with the property deal.'

'Can't imagine they needed much convincing, seeing the price the land was snapped up for, managed to get it for a song with all parties in a rush to sell,' Danny said. 'It's certain to bring in by far the biggest return, making the winnings on that screen look like loose change.'

'Howard just needed to pen the punters methods down somewhere,' Clive said.

Danny recalled Howard's laptop with lid down on his desk. It had been marked property of the BHA. In the eyes of the ruling body, Case Twelve was closed. Howard wouldn't dare put any of his case work or findings for XII on the laptop and there was no written evidence in the lounge.

He must've stored it all in the secret room. The answers were all in there until the killer cleared the place out. It made the aerial photo of Ely Park in his pocket feel even more significant.

Danny pulled out the photo. He knew this would place him at the murder scene but he was already in too deep. 'Did Howard show you this?'

Clive looked at the image and then turned it over to see the columns of figures and the two concentric arcs. He shook his head. 'No. Why?'

'When did Howard reveal he'd made the vital breakthrough on XII?'

'He called me in the train on our way to the final Ely meeting to say he knew everything,' Clive said. 'We arranged to meet up that afternoon. That's why I didn't want you turning up getting in the way.'

Danny wondered if the killer was also on the train. 'Was anyone else listening in?'

'I didn't say much about the case, understandably as I was with Jacob Rice, the man who ordered it shut,' Clive recalled. 'In all the years I'd know Howard, I'd never heard him sound so excited. It's like he'd saved the sport.'

'What time was this?' Danny asked.

'Eleven-ish.'

'Look at the time and date that image was taken from a drone flying over the course,' Danny said. 'Eight forty two. He'd clearly flown it, downloaded the image and returned to Somerset. That image is what made Howard excited.'

Clive held the image into the light. 'Can't see why. Where did you find this, again?'

'Howard had sealed off a spare bedroom in his house.'

'You went!'

'I had to,' Danny said.

'Was Howard alive?'

'Yes,' Danny said. 'On the first visit.'

'You went back.'

'I had to,' Danny repeated. 'There was some unfinished …
business.'

'Please tell me you didn't—'

'No, but I saw him … there. When you see something like
that, it never leaves you.'

Clive cursed. 'I warned you not to go.'

'That's a bit rich, you'd arranged to meet him later.'

Clive grunted. 'Can I keep this?'

Danny swiped it from Clive's hand. 'I'm not done with it.'

Danny pictured the red XII. The code name used only by
Clive and Howard.

Danny removed the badge from his jacket.

'Unlike the photo, this members badge exchanged hands at
the place where he'd painted the red XII. Howard clearly intended
this for the only other person who knew of the numerals true
meaning. I'll let you keep this.'

He handed over the maroon enamel and metal badge.

Clive held it in his palm.

'Are you sure?'

'Howard would've wanted it this way.'

'What is it?'

'A clue he left behind in his final seconds alive,' Danny
said. 'Most people would try praying or phoning loved ones,
Howard clearly felt fishing this badge out from the bowl was a
better use of his precious time.'

'It must be important then,' Clive said softly, as if mind
elsewhere. He put on his reading specs. 'Middlesex County Racing
Club.'

'The only track in Middlesex is Kempton,' Danny
explained. 'A track that's shutting down to free up land for housing
stock near a capital city. Ring any bells?'

'The Kempton deal has nothing to do with any betting
scam.'

'I know,' Danny said. 'I never said it did, but given that Howard didn't have any badges for either Cardiff or Ely races, I reckon he felt that badge was his only way of communicating to the world that his death was linked to the Ely sale.'

Clive now seemed more interested in the black and red striped cord threaded through the tiny gold loop in the badge. He started to scratch it. Danny presumed it was a nervous thing, like the pen tapping.

'Has your insider heard whether this place has granted a new track for South Wales?' Danny asked.

Clive shook his head. 'I only have an insider in the integrity department not the licensing one.'

Clive stopped scratching the cord and suddenly looked as if he'd just remembered he'd left the gas on. He then typed something into the phone on his desk.

'What are you doing?'

'It's time for you to vanish.'

'What have you seen?'

Clive showed his nails by splaying fingers like a hand model. There was dirt under them.

'So? Wash them.'

'Oh, I will, it's dried blood,' Clive said. 'How could Howard give you this if he held it as he died?'

'It exchanged hands,' Danny said, 'I never said one of them was cold at the time.'

'Tell me you didn't steal from a dead man.'

'It was no longer any use to him. Anyway, he wanted this to get to you! He chose every badge for a reason, that's what he told me,' Danny said, 'including this one, particularly this one.'

'Because his killer was linked to the Ely sale?'

'And the White Turf Group,' Danny said. 'It always comes back to them.'

'How do I know it wasn't you who killed Howard?'

'It might've been an accident,' Danny said, recalling Howard stumbling forward.

'You'd have to be pretty clumsy to get stabbed five times.'

'What?' Danny asked, tilting his head slightly. 'He was stabbed?'

Clive nodded. 'Don't you watch the news?'

'Why should I? They're wind-up merchants, it's never good news,' Danny said. 'We're definitely talking about Howard and not Larry, now?'

'Howard was killed by stab wounds to the neck and chest,' Clive explained. 'You pickpocketed this badge from the body, you must've seen the blood.'

'Oh, thank the lord,' escaped Danny's lips as he felt a palpable weight of guilt lift from his whole body.

'I'm glad someone's pleased,' Clive said, frowning.

'I didn't mean—' Danny said and thought it best not to dig a deeper hole. 'It's just the killer meant for Howard's secret to go to the grave with him. But it didn't, we've still got the badge and the photo.'

Suddenly, Clive's phone buzzed into life on the desk.

They both flinched, stared at the phone and then each other.

Clive checked the number. 'It's reception.' He swallowed and then answered, 'Hello? What is it? I'm busy.' He grimaced at the answer. 'What do they want?'

'Police?' Danny mouthed.

Clive nodded briefly.

'Can it wait five?' Clive asked, already picking Howard's blood from his nails. 'Very well ... no don't, I'll come down to show them up, they'll only get lost.'

As Clive stood and came from behind his desk, he signed the call off with. 'I won't be a minute.'

Clive looked sick, skin pallid and waxy.

'Keep cool,' Danny said. 'You were expecting them for routine questioning, you're his boss.'

'I know,' Clive said, clearing his throat.

'So why are you looking like you've got something to hide?' Danny said.

As Clive paced to the door, Danny saw he was wearing tan leather shoes with gleaming buckles. He'd seen the same from behind the bushes on the garden path.

Danny now knew it was Clive Napier that had left the murder scene that morning. Perhaps Clive did have something to hide?

'Why did you claim "Howard's dead" as you ran from there?'

125

'It's just an expression. I didn't know he was actually dead, how could I as the old sod wasn't answering the front or back door after I'd rushed all the way there to hear his discovery,' Clive said. 'I was angry and I must've said something like, "Howard's a dead man", it's just a figure of speech. How the hell did you know … never mind, that can wait. Now when I come back, I want you gone!' Clive shoved the badge deep into his pocket.

'Don't you worry about that.'

'And leave the back way, there's a fire exit at the end of the corridor turning left out of here.'

'I know.'

Clive shook his head, as if twigging how Danny had bypassed the front desk.

'If you snitch on me, telling them I was there at the murder scene, I'll say the same about you when I'm dragged in for questioning,' Danny said. 'I saw you leave, saying "Howard's dead".'

'It's a bloody expression, I was angry that he wasn't answering both the front and back doors.'

Danny recalled the banging on the kitchen door which made him leave.

'Your nails,' Danny said.

'Shit!' Clive said as he left the room in a fluster, putting his hands in his pockets, too.

When he could no longer hear footsteps along the corridor outside, Danny turned Clive's phone around. It's screen lit up. He saw the calendar app was open. He checked the date of Howard's murder. It had been left blank, just like Howard's wall calendar.

Clive had tapped something into the phone when Danny mentioned the possible theory of a replacement track for Ely. He checked today's date and saw an entry that read *Sir Benfro*. The flashing cursor suggested it was a new entry still to be saved into the box.

Sir Benfro?

The name rang a bell. Was he a friend of Sir Jacob Rice?

Danny flicked off the phone. He guessed there wouldn't be much small talk between Clive and the detectives in a public area. Clive would do well to speak at all and it would take less than a minute to ride a lift four floors there and back.

Danny rushed for the door. As he hurried down the corridor towards the stairwell and fire exit, he heard the soft ping of the lift door opening behind.

Danny didn't look back and slowed his pace. He didn't want anyone to think he was in a hurry to get away.

He heard the thud of several footsteps behind. He could see the way-out sign, agonisingly close. He braced himself for a deep booming voice call out, 'Excuse me, sir. Can we just have a minute of your time?'

He must look like a BHA employee and they'd probably want to question as many of Howard Watkins' colleagues as possible.

But all he heard was Clive stuttering, 'Come in, please, take a seat.'

The door clicked shut again and the corridor fell silent. Danny breathed out. Looking back, he was about to say, 'Thank fuck for that,' when he saw they'd posted a uniformed officer to guard the door.

They wouldn't do that just for routine questioning, Danny reckoned.

Did they suspect Clive might do a runner?

The officer slowly turned his head to stare in Danny's direction.

Danny was unsure what would look least suspicious. He just gave a pathetic half-wave.

The officer turned to face the wall, as if embarrassed for Danny. Most law abiding citizens would act nervy around them, he reckoned, as he fled down the steps two at a time.

Danny exited the metal fire door on ground level. He couldn't get out there quick enough.

When he climbed into his Honda in the car park to the rear, there were no squad cars there. They must've parked up someplace else.

Danny felt safe enough to hang fire and lock eyes on the only BMW parked there. The adrenalin from narrowly missing an interrogation had felt like a sugar rush. But sitting out there in comparative safety, he soon felt flat and tired.

Suddenly, the rush came back. Napier had left the building.

Danny simply couldn't lose him now. He had this one chance to be led to Sir Benfro, who'd suddenly entered the frame after Clive had been shown the red badge.

CHAPTER 14

Danny's feet hovered over the clutch and accelerator pedals as his eyes ducked from under the cover of the sunshield to see Clive climbing into the red BMW opposite.

He watched as the BMW headed for the car park exit before turning right into the flow of traffic on High Holborn. Safely out of view Danny pulled away and turned right in pursuit.

For hours Danny trod the fine line between staying close enough to keep the BMW in eyeshot yet far enough not to fill Napier's mirrors.

Staying mostly above eighty in the right lane of the M4 westbound, they had soon cut through Berkshire, Gloucestershire and then Monmouthshire.

Where the hell did this Sir Benfro live?

They crossed the swirling, brown waters of the River Severn on the new bridge and still showed no signs of branching off a slip road as they sped by the *Croeso I Gymru* sign welcoming visitors to Wales.

The meeting with Sir Benfro was clearly important enough to waste a whole day getting there and back. He began to wonder whether it was another code name between the head and his deputy, similar to XII.

When the journey had stretched beyond Cardiff and the two-lane bottleneck by Port Talbot, he found it increasingly harder to follow unnoticed.

Suddenly, as they left Carmarthenshire, Danny slapped the steering wheel as he looked across at the big white road sign that read *Croeso i SIR BENFRO* above *Welcome to Pembrokeshire*.

No wonder the name sounded familiar. He'd spent weeks on holiday in mobile homes down this way as a kid.

His mind's eye was filled with snapshots of sun-bleached memories on the sandy beaches at Saundersfoot, Manorbier and Tenby, before packing up to grab the best seats for a bad Elvis tribute act and bingo in the club house.

Despite barely being able to see over the Formica tables, he was already marking six books per game with his favourite blobber. His Mam reckoned he had the makings of a maths prodigy. Looking back, his Dad seemed more reserved in his outlook. Danny now reckoned that was the moment his father first saw something of the gambling self in his son. He'd probably smelt trouble ahead. He'd be proven right.

Clive was clearly more familiar with the Welsh name for the county. Danny suspected he'd also been here before.

Their progress slowed on the approach to the harbour resort of Tenby, as popular as it was picturesque.

Tracking the BMW, Danny sunk lower in his seat as they dipped under the grey-bricked viaduct on the outskirts and then climbed back up towards the medieval defensive walls surrounding the old town.

As the through road banked a sharp right, he watched Clive turn off left and follow the west wall round to the sea front. He was grateful there were no tourist buses blocking the way at this time of year.

Danny had kept close enough range to see Clive then follow the bend right into The Esplanade lined with tall Georgian hotels looking down over the sweeping golden sands of the South Beach stretching right round to the monastery on Caldey Island. He'd heard on the local news it had been voted the best beach in Europe again. He only needed one look to see why.

He'd now caught up enough to see the backend of the BMW disappear into a side street off the bracing front.

Danny kept low as he drove by and parked further down a street crammed with Bed and Breakfasts, all with vacancy signs hanging in the windows.

A gust stole his breath as he stepped from his stuffy car. He held back there to see Clive return to the sea front.

Continuing the pursuit on foot, he looked through the black railings high up on the craggy red-grey granite of the towering cliff face down over the great expanse of windswept sand, almost deserted except for a few dog walkers and metal detectorists dotted about. It was even more impressive than he'd remembered. He made a note to make the time to bring Meg, Jack and Cerys on their first summer holiday together there.

Reaching the end of The Esplanade, Clive followed the road back round to the left in the direction from where they'd arrived.

Fearing he'd lose the target, Danny quickened his stride. But when he turned to walk alongside the west wall, Clive was nowhere to be seen.

Danny cursed. He'd come all that way only to lose him in the final few yards. He still continued along the west wall, glancing through the tall arched gateway that led on to a cobbled stretch known as The Paragon but there was no sign of Napier anywhere. He'd vanished. Danny wished he hadn't given Clive so much slack having feared he'd scare him off if spotted.

Danny carried on following the wall, hopes fading with every step. Up ahead, he saw a familiar semicircular gatehouse protruding from the town wall, the Five Arches.

Stepping under the shadowy second arch, he saw no sign of Napier along St George's Street within the old part of the town facing him.

Surely Clive hadn't had the time to turn off into Upper or Lower Frog Street crossing St George's Street a good forty yards ahead.

Walking under the six feet of solid rubble stone, he suddenly froze at the sound of two male voices.

Despite the hollow echo, Danny swore he recognised both of them. Clive was definitely one, albeit deeper and muffled under there.

The meet-up had clearly been arranged for the middle arch the other side of this thick pillar.

Back pressed hard to the prickly cold of the second arch's wall, Danny shut his eyes and tried to focus on the voices, filtering out the distant laughter from a small pub just inside the west wall.

'What the hell do you think you were playing at?' Danny heard Clive say.

'I could say the same,' the other voice replied in a local accent. But he couldn't place exactly where he'd heard it before. 'I get the text saying you want to meet and this is the kind of greeting I get for coming out.'

'Howard Watkins is dead,' Clive said.

'I know, I can read,' came the reply. 'It was all over *The Racing Life*. I'm afraid you've had a wasted journey.'

Danny grimaced. If Clive came away with nothing, there was every chance he would too.

'Not when I know you did it,' Clive said.

'Why are you here pointing the finger now?'

'For Christ's sake, you're on the Ely Park Board of Directors and you're the face of Tenby,' Clive said. 'At Ely's free bar, you wouldn't shut up about your plans for a racetrack here.'

'Which means nothing.'

'Which means,' Clive replied pointedly as if already losing patience, 'you have both the motive and the means to convince the other board members to vote in favour of selling the land for housing.'

'Bullshit Clive, why the hell would I go through all that in the slim chance a substitute track would be granted a licence here.'

'I just know.'

'You heard rumours floating about the office?' the voice asked.

'I heard it from Howard, he left a message yesterday morning.'

'Howard was already dead by then. Are you hearing voices beyond the grave now? That explains a lot.'

'Howard left a farewell message behind that was meant for me.'

Danny fished in his pocket and felt for the small enamel badge but then realised he'd gifted it to Clive, who it had been intended for, in his office.

Time telescoped back to that moment he'd found the badge. The moment his whole world stood still. Knees buckling at the sight of Howard Watkins face down in his own blood.

'A replacement all-weather circuit is being discussed for near Newmarket is a consequence of Kempton Park closing,' Clive said. 'You must've known Ely's demise was your chance to get the same for Tenby.'

'And Howard is your reliable source?' There was some false, nervy laughter and then what sounded like a scuffle. 'He looked a mess when he was alive; Christ knows what he looked like when they found him.'

'Don't you say another word,' Clive replied, voice shaking with rage. 'I'm on to you.'

132

'For what?' the man replied. 'Encouraging the sale of land to be used for the much-needed supply of housing? I'd expect a MBE, if I had.'

'Oh that's just the start,' Clive said. 'You see that mess you describe also found out that whoever was behind pushing the sale was also behind both the betting scam in Case Twelve that threatened to riddle our sport with corruption and the deaths of both Larry Wallace and Howard himself.'

'You can't pin any of this on me.'

'You try me.'

Danny heard echoing footsteps. Inside the town walls, he saw the back of a stocky man in shirt and jeans walking away from the arches. He pressed his back flat to the rough stone wall in case the man glanced back.

Off to his right, Danny then saw Clive walk by the second arch heading back in the direction of his car.

Danny didn't know which way to go. Feeling he wouldn't get any more from Clive, he headed inside the west wall.

He chased after the stocky man, wincing from every stride as he tried to keep up along St George's Street.

When Danny emerged on to Tudor Square, the man had already vanished, despite there being only a handful of pedestrians and taxis on the street. Standing under the towering spire of Tenby church, Danny's alert eyes scanned the square, suspecting the man had snuck into one of the shops or restaurants lining either side of the through road.

It's then Danny saw a shadow shrink to nothing on the red and blue face of the Lifeboat Tavern by an alley on the far side of the square.

The man had clearly stopped in the alley to eye Danny's next move.

He sprinted across the square and turned into the narrow alley that funnelled salty blasts of air over his flushed cheeks as he stepped down the narrow cobbled path leading to the harbour looking out over North Beach.

Reaching for the bottom step he was about to bank right when he felt something hard connect his shin with a splintering blow.

He didn't even have time to look down as he was propelled headlong towards the sloping harbour wall along Bridge Street.

Danny's instinct as a jump jockey kicked in to lessen the shuddering impact onto the tarmac of the lane. He relaxed his body and twisted in the air to land with a roll. He led with the shoulder and flipped over, somehow finishing on his backside near the waist-high stone wall.

At least the pain shooting up his shin briefly distracted him from a bruised back and legs from the Ely fall.

Danny scrambled to his feet and turned to see the arches man in shirt and jeans doubled over rubbing his calf. He'd clearly used his leg as a tripwire.

Danny staggered over and shoved the man's shoulders to right him. His strong hand then pinned the man's neck to the wall of a terraced cottage. He made a ball with his other fist, locked and aimed on the man's face.

'I know you, you're that mayor,' Danny said. He eased his grip slightly as the man gasped for air. 'You came up to Clive and me on Ely platform.'

'I wish I hadn't,' the man wheezed. He reached into the pocket of his jeans.

Danny's grip tightened again. 'Hands where I can see them.'

'My inhaler,' the man begged.

Danny didn't want another death on his hands, least of all a dignitary in broad daylight. He let go completely and stepped back.

The man produced a blue inhaler similar to the one Danny had as a child. By the time he'd left for Lambourn, his asthma had luckily gone.

The man filled his lungs with a few puffs on the spray. Soon his breathing slowed and the panic had subsided.

'What's the mayor of Cardiff doing down here?'

'I'm Mayor of Tenby,' the man replied. 'Clive never said where I'm from.'

'I just assumed.'

The man grimaced as he ran a hand down his leg again.

'You can't blame me for that, you stuck it out.'

'What do you want, Danny?'

'Clive Napier left his busy office in London and travelled right across Britain to meet you but left with nothing,' Danny said, 'I don't give up so easy.'

'Follow me,' the man said and headed down the narrow lane. 'It's Reece by the way.'

'I remember,' Danny said. 'And you clearly know me.'

'I'm a racing fan, enough of a fan for me to shell out the training fees for a promising novice chaser called Moonbow down to run at Ludlow in two days, trainer says he's a good thing.' Reece smiled briefly. 'Clive reckoned Howard knew it all about the game but I reckon I'd have given him a good ... well, I might have done,' Reece said, voice trailing off, as he became aware of how petty that sounded now Howard was dead.

Together, they strolled down Bridge Street to the stone jetty of the working harbour by small huts selling tickets for fishing trips and island cruises, though the shutters were firmly down for winter.

They both looked beyond the piles of lobster pots out at the many fishing trawlers, sailing boats and even a dinghy moored by chains and set in the wet sand.

A fisherman was piling plastic boxes on the deck of one and a group of youngsters in black wetsuits were heading to the open beach with surfboards, while a man was tinkering with the engine of a speedboat.

Settling on a bench, Danny looked up at the Georgian houses in glowing pastel shades of pink, yellow and blue lit up by the winter sun and high above the North Beach.

He could see why it was reportedly the most photographed shot in Wales. Yet it was peaceful, serene if it weren't for the laughing seagulls.

'Quite something isn't it, the jewel in Pembrokeshire's crown?' Reece said. 'No wonder writers like George Eliot and Roald Dahl once stayed here. It's even better when the place is teeming with life, tourists swarming round ice-cream stalls and tables outside the pubs.'

Danny's nostrils were pricked by the sweet smell of seaweed carried on the air as he stared over at the outcrop Goskar Rock rising up from beach. He had to remind himself he hadn't come there for the sights.

'Why do it?' Danny broke the silence.

'Do what?' Reece asked back, shifting his weight to face Danny.

'In the third arch back there, Clive accused you with the means and motive to push the Ely sale through.'

'As a board member, I can cast *one* vote and for what it's worth I voted against the sale.'

'But your dream is to open a track here.'

'I love this place but I love racing more.'

'I don't believe that for one second, *Mayor*.'

'But you *can* believe we'd get planning permission approved for a racecourse in a medieval town? The only other sport that takes up that kind of space is golf,' Reece said, tilting his head slightly. 'You'd do well to put up a garden shed without questions being asked round here. I'm afraid you turned the wrong way out of the Five Arches.'

'It can't be Clive behind it all.'

'Why are you so certain?'

'Why would he drive over five hours to confront you? He'd know it would be a wasted trip before he left High Holborn.'

'If you commit a crime what would you hope happens?' Reece said. 'The best outcome you could hear?'

'They shut the case.'

'That would lead to a lifetime of fearing they might open it again for a relook,' Reece said. 'No, the best outcome is that another gets wrongly sent down for it.'

'So he was looking to frame you,' Danny reasoned. 'If you've nothing to hide Reece, why run from him?'

'He grabbed me, not a good look for a mayor to be caught fighting on my own patch. "An upstanding pillar of the community witnessed in brawl", I can see the headline in the *Tenby Observer* now.'

Danny could see Reece put his hands on the bench as if to push himself up. He shot an arm out as a barrier. 'I'm not done.'

'Look, it's true I've sent myself off to sleep countless times dreaming of this place seeing the return of racing to the area. My hopes faded when Ffos Las was granted a licence in Carmarthenshire. I knew then the rulers wouldn't hand another one out to west Wales.

But when I saw you successfully campaign for the rebirth of a once-thriving track at Ely my energy and enthusiasm returned.'

'Are you saying there was a track here in the past,' Danny asked. 'And you reckoned there wasn't the space.'

'The track back then was near the small village called New Hedges outside Tenby.'

'What's stopping them replacing one there now?'

'We're in the UK's largest coastal park, the land is protected.'

'You're mayor,' Danny said. 'You must know the right people in planning.'

'You're right, I am a mayor – but I'm not a miracle worker. If you want a fete opening or unveiling a plaque maybe,' Reece replied. 'It's mostly a ceremonial role. In any case, as you can see, this place is seasonal. The population of five thousand multiplies by a factor of ten in the summer. A racecourse needs year-round turnover.'

Danny looked around. They were alone. It's as if the town was recharging its batteries ready for the hustle and bustle of the summer holiday season.

'No, the man you're after went the other side of the arches. He's not to be trusted, Danny.'

Perhaps I was wrong, Danny thought, maybe the Middlesex badge didn't refer to Kempton at all.

Reece chuckled to himself. 'My great-uncle Anthony used to recount stories about the Tenby racing scene, that's what first got me hooked. I used to call him my great, great-uncle,' he said and smiled again. 'He used to go there as a kid, you see. Ely Park wasn't the only thriving National Hunt racetrack in nineteenth-century Wales.'

Danny recalled Howard mentioning there had been over sixteen hundred tracks that had come and gone. He wondered if there had been a Tenby badge in the cranberry bowl.

Reece continued, 'That one-and-a-half mile track of flat country ground was a hotbed for jumping talent. Anthony used to get in free by hopping over the hedge of Three Chimneys cottage which happened to share the entrance to the track. I will never forget my uncle's eyes lighting up when he relived the likes of legendary local mare Fairy Queen, who won a steeplechase there

137

by a mile back in 1894, carrying twelve stone three pounds, and then managed to carry thirteen stone six pounds to win the Stewards Plate, followed under an hour later by a win in the Visitor's Hurdle. She ended up netting six wins in just thirteen days. They don't make them like that anymore.'

'I'd thought Powder Keg was tough.'

'We even had a top local trainer. David Harrison – his yard was on Upper Frog Street.'

'Where the Tenby bookies are found today?'

Reece nodded. 'Just up from there. Uncle recalled watching Harrison's string stretch out in gallop work along South Beach. Must've been quite a sight at first light. He trained Lancashire Chase winner Avenger, who went on to finish runner-up to the mighty Golden Miller in the Cheltenham Gold Cup no less. It helped put Tenby races on the map. That was until they shut the gates at Three Chimneys cottage for the final time in 'thirty-six, such a great shame, a travesty in my view.'

Danny looked across to see anger in those green eyes. The motive to rebirth the track was definitely there.

Reece's breath began to rattle again. He took another puff on the inhaler.

'Bet you were jealous of the success story of Ely Park's revival,' Danny said.

'Except for the shutting down part,' Reece replied.

'Don't be so sure history wouldn't repeat itself at Tenby as well,' Danny replied. 'You said yourself this place goes to sleep most of the year.'

'It wasn't the location that proved Tenby racetrack's downfall first time around,' Reece explained. He shifted his weight on the bench to eye Danny again. 'In 1927, the racing world was rocked by a scandal at Tenby races – claimed as the biggest in National Hunt history – that became known as The Oyster Maid Coup. It scared off many from going to the track, including Uncle Anthony. It happened in a low-grade hurdle race on a rainy, sleety afternoon there. A small field lined up, with Harrison saddling both the hot-favourite Bubbly at two-to-five and an outsider, Oyster Maid. They used a tic-tac man to relay off-course bets placed with the illegal bookies' runners in seedy bars and on street corners around the country. The tic-tac man used to stand on Mansion Hill about half a mile away from the track where there was a phone. Inexplicably, this low-grade race was subject to floods of off-course bets just before the off, hundreds there were, all for the outsider – the supposed no-hoper – via bookies' runners and telephone bets. Unfortunately, the forecast weather had made visibility so bad, the tic-tac man on the hill couldn't tell the course bookies to shorten the on-course odds, which all bookies had to pay out on. When the runners emerged from the gloom on the final lap, there were only two horses in contention. The result was a one-two for Harrison but not the way the betting odds had forecast. Oyster Maid was driven clear at odds of over sixteen to one. Illegal bookies up and down the land were crying foul as they forked out the equivalent of millions in today's money.'

'And your uncle never went again, after this? Was he found to be part of the coup and warned off?' Danny said.

'Scared off,' Reece corrected. 'After the scandal, the name Tenby Racetrack left a bad taste in the mouth of the off-course bookies that'd got their fingers burnt by the coup. When bookies stopped turning up and taking bets, the punters began to stay away. They could never pin down the culprits. Less than a decade later, Tenby was no more. I feel sad for the locals who needed the passing trade.'

'I know the feeling,' Danny said. 'I need my nearest track open for the yard to survive. The travelling costs are crippling for an operation my size.'

'Maybe the past was repeating itself in the present,' Reece suggested.

'Eh?'

'Perhaps a similar scandal was linked to Ely Park,' Reece said.

'Whatever has gone on at Ely, Howard reckoned it could happen elsewhere. He told me it could bring down racing as a betting sport,' Danny said. 'One more thing, have you heard of the White Turf Group?'

Reece took another puff of his inhaler.

'You okay? I'm not making you stressed?'

Looking ahead, Reece replied, 'No, never heard of them.'

'I'm surprised, you being a board member,' Danny said, 'they're the consortium behind the purchase of Ely.'

'Again, I was voted on to the board for my love of racing,' Reece said. 'Not to sell the place.'

Danny stood. 'I'll leave you in peace. I'm sorry you had to face Clive earlier.'

'Don't be,' Reece said. 'I'm just glad I didn't end up like Larry and Howard.'

They parted with a shake of hands. Returning to his car, he saved going full circle by taking a shortcut along a small winding lane of fisherman's cottages that led to The Paragon and Esplanade.

When he saw an empty space where the red BMW had been any sense of urgency vanished. As he'd feared Clive was already gone.

There was no chance he'd catch him up given the speed he'd averaged on the way there.

Danny turned to look out at the sea sparkling in the cold winter sun.

However many times he'd come up here, the impact would never fade.

He could picture David Harrison's imposing steeplechasers led by Avenger, feet slapping the wet sand as they galloped in full stride single file along the water's edge nearly a century ago.

One majestic force of nature meeting another, Danny thought, grinning.

A barrel-chested seagull the size of a small dog had finished pecking at a fag packet and was strutting about like he was the real mayor of this town, sharp orange eyes staring Danny down. Clearly a diet of ice cream, chips and fags worked well for gulls, he thought.

From nowhere Danny heard footsteps. As he turned he suddenly felt a hand push his chest. He then felt feet stamp down on the toes of his trainers to anchor him to the pavement.

Danny couldn't stop his upper body being forced back to hang over the precipice. He felt the rounded ends of the spearheaded finials topping the railing dig into the lumbar region of his back.

'What did he say to you?' came a voice.

Danny beat gravity to lift his head enough to see the face looking back. Clive Napier.

140

Clive held him there, suspended over the cliff top, fiery eyed, like he was ready to let go.

'You came after the wrong man,' Danny grunted. 'P-p-please, rein me in.'

'You're like a bad smell that won't go away.'

He made the mistake of looking down at the dizzying drop to jagged rocks far below. It was only his core strength and balance as a jockey that saved his spine from snapping.

He felt sick from the loss of control, the vulnerability. His life was in the hands of the man who put him there.

'Reece is the only man with the means and motive to convince the other board members to sell Ely.'

'Reece didn't have the motive,' Danny wheezed, gulping for air as he struggled to fill his lungs. His stomach muscles began to shake and cramp from the strain.

'Again, what did he say?'

'Pull me back and I'll say. The hotels behind, they're watching.'

'It's winter, they're empty.'

'I can't breathe.'

Danny felt Clive tighten his grip on his jacket. He didn't know whether that was good or bad.

Suddenly he felt the pull of Clive's white-knuckled hands and was returned to the safety of the paved Esplanade.

Danny staggered a few steps away from the railing to be sure.

'Well?' Clive asked. His eyes looked sad, lifeless, like part of him had given up, not just on Case XII, but on life itself.

Danny gagged for air. 'He blames you for everything.'

'He's lying,' Clive said.

'Well, I know one of you is.'

'I'm no killer,' Clive said.

'You've a funny way of showing it.'

'Reece has played both of us for fools,' Clive said. 'He has the means to convince the board.'

'But not the motive,' Danny repeated, and turned to look along the row of imposing white Georgian hotels facing the distant rumbling sea. 'Reece would never get a racetrack by town planning, there's barely enough room for parking in Tenby.'

141

'Are you sure about that?' Clive asked, still facing seaward. 'You're looking at this the wrong way.' He then spread his arms like a conductor. 'There's Reece's motive for you.'

'Out there,' Danny whispered.

'He's willing to sacrifice the cash cow of a betting fraud and a seat at the board of Ely Park to realise his Tenby dream.'

'Did Howard even hint at this before his death?'

'You've seen the badge,' Clive said, removing it from his pocket. 'With this Middlesex badge it's as if he was talking directly to me.'

Danny looked back over the windswept sands to the dunes and golf course behind. 'I'd been looking at it since I came but I simply didn't see it.'

Clive explained, 'Reece wouldn't need planning permission as Mother Nature has already built it for him. The beach even has one of the world's largest tidal ranges, allowing more than enough time to host a seven-race meeting between low and high tides. Laytown in Ireland remains popular after over a hundred and forty years of beach racing under rules over six and seven furlongs on the strand in County Meath.

'You'd get a mile and two on that stretch easy,' Danny replied.

'And Tenby being a holiday hotspot will help. On hot summer afternoons, imagine the crowds it would get on the beach and from high up here.'

'Reece said he'd never heard of the White Turf Group,' Danny said.

'You believing him is the only thing that surprises me about Reece lying,' Clive said. 'He drove the sale through Danny.'

Should've named it the Golden Turf Group, Danny thought, scanning the glorious stretch of sand.

'Where the hell do you think the mayor went? Do you know his address?'

Clive shook his head. 'We didn't meet under the arches for the sightseeing. He wouldn't go back to his address anyway, not immediately.'

'Where then?'

'Anywhere,' Clive said. 'Is there a house in this town that would turn away an upstanding mayor when he came knocking? He's gone for today Danny. Give up, go home.'

'I've seen another side to you since coming here,' Danny said. 'I heard you rough up Reece in the arch and then you nearly throw me over there.'

'I pinned your feet down,' Clive explained. 'You weren't going anywhere, unless you took me with you, which might've been for the best.'

'Why are you being like this?'

'If you think I killed Howard, you don't know the first thing about what I'm like.' Clive dropped his weight on one of the many benches lining the sea front. He blew hard and pinched the bridge of his nose. 'I've been under pressure, you see my wife … my love.'

'You only missed a birthday,' Danny said. 'She'll forgive you, make it up to her on the next one.'

'I won't!' Clive said. 'This'll be her last one … she has cancer … stage three breast cancer.'

Danny was shocked into silence. 'Oh shit, Clive, I—'

'I know you didn't know,' Clive said. 'Why should you? I've kept it from everyone. It's been hell. I've tried to bury myself in work, but now my only true friend among the handicappers is also gone. And this pain right between my eyes just won't go away, it just won't. I can't cope I honestly can't go on. What do I do? She wants me at home. She needs me there, now more than ever.'

He began to sob.

Danny could see the man was on the brink. This was no act. Thinking back he could see the cracks forming when the police called. He was now a broken man.

He understood now why he'd been so angry at missing his wife's birthday. It would be their last together.

'I'm … I'm sorry,' Danny said and put a hand on Clive's shaking shoulder. 'Really I am. There's help out there, there must be. You don't need to face this alone.'

Clive blew his nose. 'I haven't cried in years, must be the sea air.' He let out a snotty laugh.

Danny said, 'I think you need to go home too, she needs you, be there for her. I've learnt that the hard way.'

Clive nodded. 'I guess you're right.'

'Hang in there leave this with me, Reece won't get away with this.'

'Remember Danny, means and motive.'

Danny headed back to his car.

Of the four people that definitely knew about Case XII, one was dead and another was broken. That left Danny and the killer. He wished he'd never been let in on Howard and Clive secret case.

Back in the driver's seat of his Honda, Danny checked his phone. He was glad there were no missed calls this time, but he had been sent a text sent from Sophie Towers' number in his contacts list. It simply read: 'I'm sorry.'

He sat there reading the same two words over and over.

'For what?' he whispered. The fact he didn't know made him uneasy.

He chucked his phone on the passenger seat and reluctantly left for the Valleys before Meg had time to get any more suspicious.

By the time Danny had returned to the seafront Clive had already gone, presumably back to where he'd moved his BMW.

CHAPTER 15

Danny was glad to be home before dark.

He checked in on his horses, and saw many had been moved to the new part which was more for recuperation than quarantine.

Several of the bolder horses stuck their heads from the stable doors, curious to greet the arrival.

'Must look like a stranger to you guys,' he said softly as he greeted the mix of flat racers and jumpers one by one. Having been distracted since Doncaster, he hadn't paid them the attention they deserved.

When he reached Pobble Beach's loose box, he heard a voice quietly muttering away.

Had Gash returned?

Danny ducked low as he crept by the half-open stable door. He slowly, quietly unbolted the top half ready to slam it shut, trapping them inside.

As he spun round, he let go of the door.

'Jordi?' Danny asked, checking his watch. 'Why are you still here?'

'I wanted leave all of them looking their best, no?' Jordi said.

'But I pay you 'til two on a Monday, I can't afford overtime right now.'

'I do this with my own time, yes?' Jordi said. 'I say sorry.'

'For what?'

'You make me head lad, Mr Rawlings,' Jordi said. 'In Spain we say, "*Bien predica quien bien vive*". I need to act like it to others.'

Danny had been surprised by Jordi and Beth both slacking in recent months.

He pinched the ear of Pobble Beach. 'Well, now these guys are coming back to more like themselves, it's time for us all to step up.'

'This one worked well,' Jordi said and then smiled. 'A P.B. for P.B.'

'I know. I'm trying to forget the way this one demolished Zebrawood, along with any real chance of Garrick investing his fortunes up here.'

'No, I worked him again this morning,' Jordi explained. 'He beat Homebird easy.'

'But he's a four-year-old,' Danny said and sighed. He had a word in Pobble Beach's ear. 'You're going to have to stop beating the rest in the yard, do you hear? It's not good for the reputation of your buddies or the morale of the yard having such a lowly rated horse ruling the gallops.'

'I'm sorry. I should've asked permission to start working them all again. It's just, they were excited to get back to work, like me.'

'I think it should be me apologising,' Danny said. He felt foolish and ashamed that he'd suspected Jordi of poisoning the horses he clearly loved after seeing the ripped feed bag in the barn.

'My job is safe?' Jordi asked, frowning.

Danny smiled. 'I don't know what this place would do without you.'

Jordi breathed out. 'Thank you, Mr Rawlings. If you need anything else doing before I leave …'

Danny turned to head for the lodge when he stopped. 'There is something. At Doncaster, heading to meet Powder Keg and Meg, I saw you put a brown paper parcel in your fleece. Can I ask, what was in it?'

Jordi's frown returned.

'You can tell me to mind my own business.'

'No, I … I need to tell you, just there never—'

'Was the right time,' came a female voice behind Danny. He looked back to see Bethan walking towards them.

From her denims she pulled what looked like a small ring from her denims and slipped it on.

'It took six months for Jordi to save up for this,' Beth said, splaying her fingers to show off the small diamond on a thin gold band.

'You're engaged?'

They both nodded nervously.

Danny laughed. 'Wow, congratulations, both of you. I didn't … I mean, I hadn't seen you together, not like that anyway, you hid it well.

'We were afraid how you'd react, having a couple working here,' Beth said.

'I can hardly judge,' Danny said, 'married to the assistant trainer.'

'Losing our jobs here would've put an end to any wedding plans. And Jordi couldn't go home as there isn't much of a racing scene in Spain, particularly since Mijas shut.'

Danny ran a hand over his scalp. 'I never even saw you wearing it around here.'

She pointed over at the sign by the entrance to the stables. 'Rule six: no jewellery to be worn by staff during work hours.'

'Explains why you both turned up late,' Danny said. 'It wasn't like either of you.'

'We felt bad, it's just he's staying with me at my parents in Rhymney, we never have any time together alone. Occasionally, we had to sneak off into the store barn for some privacy. We left a gap between us leaving there, not to get found out.'

Danny recalled Jordi shiftily leaving the store barn alone. 'I heard something fall when I came in to lock up, it wasn't rats.'

'I felt like a rat hiding there in the dark from my boss,' she said. 'Jordi had to sneak in the kitchen and get the key to unlock the barn door when he *finally* realised I was stuck in there, that's why I missed one of the gallop workouts on a final warning. It won't *ever* happen again.'

'I know,' Danny said. 'Just promise me, no more secrets, yeah?'

'Yes, Mr Rawlings,' they both replied eagerly.

'Oh, and make sure we're invited to the wedding,' Danny said. He hated weddings, but he knew Meg needed something to look forward to.

'You're already on the second table of our seating plan,' Beth said, beaming.

Danny shook Jordi's hand and kissed Beth. 'Best bit of news I've had for months.'

'We think so too,' Beth said and looked lovingly at her fiancé.

147

Danny couldn't wait to share it with Meg, who he found on the sofa in the lounge.

'Have you heard the news about Jordi and Beth?'

'Beth told me yesterday,' Meg replied quietly.

He often felt dyslexic when trying to read people but even he could see she was down about something.

'Don't let Gash get to you. He's gone, forever.'

'I haven't.' She stood and walked to the hearth, leaving her phone on the coffee table.

'He can't have texted you, our personal numbers aren't on the website.'

'It's nothing to do with him.'

'Well, I'm no fan of weddings, but I'm still pleased for them.'

'So am I.'

'What is it then?

'It's not their marriage that needs saving.'

'I thought we were good.'

'We were,' she said.

He went over. She crossed her arms.

Filling the screen was an image of Sophie and Danny kissing under an orange glow.

The selfie she'd tricked him into, Danny cringed.

'It's not what it looks like.'

'Save me the clichés Danny, I've got eyes.'

'Why the hell did she send that?'

'I'm glad she did,' she said. 'At least I can see why you were so keen to go on that camping trip down to Ely Park, save on booking a seedy hotel room I guess.'

'Think about it,' Danny protested.

'I've done little else,' she replied. 'You shagging that leggy mare while leaving an old friend behind to grope me.'

'He's no friend, I keep telling you that,' Danny said and picked up her phone. 'And I never kissed her.'

'Oh, it's been Photoshopped has it?'

'She kissed me.'

'What's the difference? Your lips are locked.'

'For that second it took her to take the photo,' Danny said. 'If she'd only filmed it you'd have seen me push her away straight after.'

'Why would she do this? To get revenge?' Meg asked. 'I don't know her. We've never even been introduced.'

'It's to get revenge on me, 'cos I blew her out that night. If she couldn't have me, no one else could.'

'At least your ego comes out well from this.'

'I tried to get her off me, just like you did with Gash,' Danny said. 'If he'd taken a photo with his hand on your thigh, I'd have believed you that it was one-way traffic.'

'Don't you dare compare the two!'

'Look, she came down to see if I was okay,' Danny explained. 'I could hardly turn her away, she'd come out in the middle of the night with hot drinks and it was her track. I was a guest down there.'

'So you felt you owed her a favour.'

'Meg, don't be so—'

'Childish? I might be the younger one in this marriage but I've got a brain and eyes,' she said and grabbed her phone. 'And this isn't the worst of it, she plans to tweet it to her twelve hundred followers. Most of them are in the racing industry. You'll be seen as the trainer no one can trust and I'll be the pathetic wife that isn't enough for you.'

He fished for his phone and turned it to show Meg. 'Look at this. Sophie sent a text apologising, she knew what she was doing, she knew the damage it would do, don't let her win,' he said. 'It wasn't even a snog, just a brief peck, wouldn't surprise me if she took this just to get back at me for slagging off her turf management after a slip I had there. How does it go ... "hell hath no fury like a woman scorned"?'

'You got that right Danny,' she screamed and stormed from the room. He heard her feet thud upstairs. He felt it best not to follow her yet.

Fingers shaking Danny texted Sophie: 'Go public with that image and you will never work again.'

Minutes later, the reply came. 'I don't intend to.'

Intend to what, Danny thought. Post the tweet or work again.

He hoped it was an empty threat. Sophie wouldn't come out of this too well either.

Danny retired to the racing office again.

Through the wall he could make out the muffled sobbing of Meg in the master bedroom next door.

He'd give her more time and space than last time.

He put the aerial photo of Ely Park on the desk.

What were you trying to tell us Howard? What secret had you discovered while studying in your hidden room?

Clive reckoned Reece was the only one with the means and motive to push the sale through. He didn't think there'd be anything to get the mayor out of hiding.

Suddenly something else he'd heard at Tenby struck home. On the jetty Reece had enthused about a horse he owned. The mayor reckoned his horse Moonbow was going to be entered for a novice chase at Ludlow tomorrow.

Danny went to *The Racing Life* website. Moonbow was among the final declarations. He clicked on the six-year-old gelding's profile. He was trained by Jamie Bunce, ridden by Tony Walters and owned by Reece Porter.

Why had he picked out Jamie Bunce as his trainer?

Moonbow was forecast to go off the five-to-four favourite. Clearly he was a leading player. At those odds, Reece would surely be tempted to turn up to lead his fancy into the winners' circle.

Clive had implied Reece was behind the White Turf Group of investors that bought up Ely land. But would Reece dare return to the scene where Larry was dumped? There was only one way to know for sure. He checked the time of the first race: 1.15 PM.

He could no longer hear anything through the wall. Perhaps Meg had cried herself to sleep.

Danny went to the filing cabinet. He reached in and picked up the accounting books. He pulled out a small bottle of whiskey he'd hidden there for times like this.

He took a swig as he sat back down.

He was curious as to why the buyers of Ely Park had chosen White Turf Group as the consortium name. If the substitute track would be on the sands of Tenby, surely yellow or gold would've been more appropriate. He searched online for the White Turf Group. He could see why the trail for Case Twelve had run cold. There was nothing online about the investors. No websites, no images, no news articles.

He did, however, see numerous mentions of White Turf. He clicked on a website and saw it was an annual race meeting held on a frozen lake in the ski resort of St Moritz since 1907. It was held on the first three Sundays each February when the ice was thick enough to bear the weight of half-tonne thoroughbreds on the compacted snow surface, along with up to ten thousand racegoers.

Clearly the Geneva-based investors were regulars to name the consortium after the festival, Danny reckoned. He saw the early declarations were out for the feature Grand Prix de St Moritz at the meeting on week Sunday. He clicked on each horse, focusing on the owners' names. Suddenly he stopped at the Irish-bred Flying Machine trained by Lucas Schmid and owned by the White Turf Group.

Greedy bastards are probably treating it as a tax deductible expense, Danny thought, that's if they're paying any in their Swiss bank accounts.

Danny was distracted by streaky blue flashes up the wall in front of him. He turned to see the blue was stronger through the curtain overlooking the driveway.

Police! Danny felt his stomach shrink. They will come for you!

He reckoned the forensics taken from Howard's house had come back with a positive match in the DNA database. Danny, however, didn't see that as a positive.

He simply couldn't be held for questioning, especially now. He needed his freedom to get justice for Larry and Howard.

He closed the browser and then the laptop. He rushed into the master bedroom.

Meg rubbed her pink eyes. 'What's happening?'

'The police are here,' Danny said. 'Did you call for them?'

'No, why would I?'

Danny had already grabbed a jacket from his closet.

'Where are you going?' she asked.

'Anywhere but here.'

'Answer the door Danny, you've done nothing wrong,' she said, now sat up. 'You promised, no more running.'

'You know I've got a phobia of them, ever since I got sent down as a kid.'

'I don't think anyone wants them to come knocking,' she said, following him along the landing. 'You still have to answer.'

Danny could hear boots the other side of the oak front door.

He put a finger to his lips and then whispered. 'I love you. I'll explain everything when I return.'

'What shall I say to them?'

'Tell them what you know.'

'But I don't know anything.'

'That's perfect.'

'Where shall I say you are?'

'I'm on a bloodstock trip or something, I'll be back to answer questions in a few days.'

'What's this about, Danny?'

'I can't say,' Danny said. 'But I need to do this, Meg. I know this is a lot to ask, but can you ask them to show ID.. at the lounge window, buys me time to slip out the back way.'

She looked confused. 'Do I have a choice?'

'Not unless you want me ending up in a prison or a morgue.'

'What have you done?'

'Nothing, but they don't know that,' Danny said. 'You might hate me right now, but you still trust me, right?'

She paused.

'Meg?'

Danny swore he saw the hint of a nod as she frowned. That was enough for him. 'Thank you, love.'

He silently crept down the stairs and turned to head for the kitchen to the rear. He flinched as there was a loud thud of a fist banging the oak of the front door.

Danny fished out a roll of twenties from a jam jar set aside for petty cash behind the bleach under the sink. He'd need at least this for transport and food. No way was he going to take the Honda if the police would be on the lookout.

He stepped out into the icy cold. He shut the door and ran upslope, burying himself in the black cloak of night.

Far enough to feel safe, he turned and looked down at the rectangle of warm light in the kitchen he'd just left.

He saw Meg enter, followed by two men, one suited, the other in uniform.

He saw Meg's lips move as she tied her hair back.

Danny felt like he'd let her down, again. He desperately wanted to reach out, talk to her. Explain everything. Why he had to leave. That he wasn't a coward.

He was home yet he now felt like an outsider looking in.

Perhaps she was right, Danny thought, I run at the first sight of trouble.

But he needed his freedom to right the wrongs. With his DNA at the scene they would surely apply to keep him locked up for forty-eight hours at least and then charge him for tampering with a crime scene for starters.

He watched intently as she then turned to the sink beneath the window facing him. Pouring a glass of water, she looked directly ahead. Her eyes lacked focus as she stared out into the night. It's as if she couldn't see him but she could sense he was still there.

She mouthed. 'It's okay.'

She then turned and shepherded the officers into the lounge.

Danny also turned and began the climb, guided by the glacier-blue light from the full moon that picked out the treetops of the wooded copse by the ridge.

Cresting the rise at the top, Danny shivered as his skin crawled under just a thin jacket and t-shirt. He didn't look back.

He paced down to the Rhymney Road at the edge of the Silver Belle Estate. He followed the road until finding a signal on his phone strong enough to order a taxi to the train station. From there, he booked a return ticket to Ludlow.

Reece Porter wasn't going to fool him this time.

CHAPTER 16

Danny stepped on to the platform at Ludlow station.

Thinking he might need to keep some cash back he ignored the taxi rank on his way to the racetrack. He bit back the pain for two miles, still feeling the effects of the Ely fall.

He hadn't had the time or forethought to pick up his owner's and trainer's badge as he ran from his home as the police arrived. He wasn't keen on using his jockey's licence for fear of his attendance being logged someplace. Instead, he resorted to paying at the turnstiles like every other punter.

His pace slowed walking by the red phone box beside the betting ring in front of the main grandstand. He didn't want to be seen staring at the place where Larry had been left for dead. But regular shifty side glances over there made him feel even more suspicious.

It would've been too open to stab Larry there, Danny reckoned, even in the dark after racing. Larry must've been dumped there unconscious. He kept his distance, aware he'd already left prints and DNA at one murder scene.

He imagined the killer dragging Larry's skewered body there. It would take plenty of muscle to lump what effectively was dead weight.

Mayor Reece Porter could've comfortably done it.

He left the restaurants and betting ring behind as he walked over the matting unfurled across the hurdle and chase tracks to help protect the grass.

A rail track and racetrack immediately either side of the grandstand enclosures meant there wasn't enough space to fit in the parade and pre-parade rings and saddling boxes. Instead, punters viewed the horses prior to the races on the infield before returning to the betting ring to wager on their fancy.

Danny had no intention of returning to the stands until Moonbow had run his race in the novices' chase that opened the card.

He snuck into the saddling enclosure among a group of syndicate owners hoping to catch the security man off-guard.

Relieved to be in, he checked a list on the wall to see where Moonbow was due to be tacked up before and unsaddled after the race. He then found a sheltered spot beyond the saddling enclosures away from stable staff and nervous connections. He didn't mind waiting. He just hoped Reece had turned out.

When the six runners filed into the parade ring and started to circle, Danny found a front-row seat and leant his weight on the white plastic railing. He watched as small groups of owners with their trainers and jockeys began to enter the ring to inspect their horses while talking race tactics and prospects.

There was, however, one notable exception. Reece Porter.

It soon became clear hot favourite Moonbow was only being represented by his trainer Jamie Bunce and jockey Tony Walters, who'd retained the ride for this switch to fences having won a hurdle race on him at Hereford last month.

Mayor Reece didn't appear the shy, retiring type, Danny thought.

Perhaps both Clive and Danny turning up on his own patch had spooked him at Tenby, or maybe he felt returning to the murder scene was pushing his luck.

When he heard the clang of the bell signalling jockeys to get the leg up, Danny felt he'd seen enough. He was determined it wouldn't be a wasted journey and hung around there for the return of the runners.

He went to the unsaddling box where Moonbow had just left and listened to the crackly racecourse commentary over the speakers dotted about.

Although the muffled words were hard to decipher under this shelter, Danny could tell by the roar of the crowd and the somewhat monotone pitch of the race call that the favourite had won by a wide margin as expected.

He listened intently as the steward declared, 'Here is the result of the one-fifteen … first number four Moonbow eleven-to-ten favourite, second number three Man The Barricades five-to-one. All six ran.'

At least Bunce might be in a better mood than when they last met, Danny thought.

Soon Danny heard footsteps grow louder. This time he wanted Bunce to be the one caught off guard. He knew the trainer would return here before the horse as the winner of every race was drug tested by the integrity department of the BHA.

As Bunce swept in carrying the tack over his arm, Danny lunged forward and grabbed the tweed sleeve. He yanked him deeper under the shelter of the box.

'Danny?!' Bunce growled. 'What is this, revenge for having a go at you in Doncaster? Fair enough, I suppose. I did act like a dick.'

'Where is he?'

'Who?'

'Your owner Reece Porter, another bad loser.'

'No show I'm afraid, first time ever,' Bunce said. 'Great shame as Moonbow hosed up easier on this switch to fences than he did over hurdles back on the fourteenth. Exciting chase prospect this one.'

'Where did Reece find the money to own horses?'

'You can't blame the man for one luxury,' Bunce replied. 'Racing is his life away from work, others go on holidays or drive fast cars. And its *horse* by the way, he only owns Moonbow. Why are you asking?'

'Has he ever been to St Moritz?'

'Like I say, he doesn't bother with holidays.'

'Bollocks,' Danny said and pushed Bunce against the cold bricks of the dividing wall.

Bunce smiled. 'I could shout for security or swat you like a fly, but I won't,' Bunce said. 'You see, I feel sorry for you Danny.'

'It didn't look that way when you came steamrollering for me at Doncaster,' Danny said.

'I had been certain Sweetshop would win the nursery.'

'Why?' Danny asked. 'He'd only won a slowly run maiden.'

'He'd been catching pigeons at home since, beating everything in sight,' Bunce said. 'Off a low mark, he rated a certainty in my eyes, until you came along and knocked him sideways going for a gap that wasn't there.'

'There was enough room for one up the rail,' Danny said. 'I got there first, that's race-riding.'

Suddenly, Danny let go of his grip as a revelation struck him. 'Where had Sweetshop won?'

'Down your place, Ely Park.'

'The bends!' Danny said, 'they're altering time.'

'Think you've got the bends, talking like that,' Bunce said. 'I know you're from Cardiff but Doctor Who isn't real.'

'Don't you see?!' Danny said and removed the drone image.

'Three factors change the time horses take to complete: pace, going and distance,' Danny said. 'The punter on a winning streak was shifting the rails on the bend to change the distance of the race. No wonder they were choosing races over seven furlongs and a mile to make sure the horses travelled the entire bend.' Danny turned the image over. 'Look! The two parallel rings, Howard already knew. He'd scribbled this down on the morning he died.'

'What made you suddenly see all this?'

'Sweetshop,' Danny said. 'I've got one the same, Pobble Beach, who was lowly rated after winning a slowly run Ely Maiden. Since then, he's been shaping like a horse better than his handicap mark on the gallops, just like yours. I was wrong all along, Zebrawood wasn't overrated, Pobble Beach was underrated.'

'You've lost me.'

'The Ely Park races won by Sweetshop and Pobble Beach were both rigged to look bad,' Danny said. 'Molehills!'

'Oh, now you're making a lot more sense,' Bunce said, rolling his eyes.

'Except they're not molehills,' Danny said, grabbing Bunce's tweed arm again.

'Do you mind if I go collect the trophy on behalf of my owner?' Bunce asked. 'I feel I've been punished enough for my outburst at Doncaster.'

'Don't you see? Pobble Beach had slipped on a small mound of earth on the bend. It wasn't a molehill but where they'd filled in the hole left by shifting a rail post.'

'Clerks are always shifting the rails to free up fresh strips of ground,' Bunce reasoned.

'But they declare the change in distance to the authorities and media,' Danny said. 'Ely Park never did. Shifting the rails out on the bend would slow the time and that would devalue the form of the race in the eyes of both the handicappers and punters.'

He could see why Sophie had come rushing over after the fall there. She was more concerned by a lawsuit than Danny's health. The clerk of the course was the only one with the authority to move the plastic railing.

'Push the rails out a few yards over an entire bend would extend the race distance by way more.' He was good with figures but had skipped enough double maths to be a stranger to geometry. He checked online for a converter. The perimeter of a semicircle was equal to pi times the radius plus two times the radius. He used the calculator on his phone. 'For every five yards they shifted the rail, the horses need to cover an extra twenty-six yards.'

'But that would only slow the race time by a few seconds,' Bunce said. 'It would only adjust the handicap marks in a race by three or four pounds.'

Danny fell quiet. Bunce had a point. There had to be something else to further manipulate the time and therefore the handicap marks.

The speakers crackled, 'Would Jamie Bunce go to the parade rings, please, Jamie Bunce to the parade ring, thank you.'

'Our time is up,' Jamie said. 'Do you honestly think Reece would be capable of changing the shape of Ely track?'

'He's on the board there,' Danny said. 'When was the last time you saw him?'

'At Hereford,' Bunce said.

'You said just now that was January the fourteenth.'

Bunce glanced at the race-card and pointed at the bracketed figure next to Moonbow's name denoting the days since his last run. 'Yes, January the fourteenth. Look.'

Danny pictured the wall calendar. The day Howard died. 'You say Reece was at Hereford to watch it?'

'He left the Ely do early especially to see his horse. It was a great afternoon from the bits I remember,' Bunce said. 'We were in hospitality. Reece could easily have ended in hospital, knocking them back he was.'

'What time did you arrive and leave?'

'What's this about Danny?'

'Tell me, now!'

'Early afternoon, left late.'

Shit!

'Were there others with you?'

'It's hospitality,' Bunce said. 'It was packed in there.'

Any amount of means and motives would always be trumped by countless alibis.

Danny had to face it, he was wrong. Reece was innocent. Was it Clive playing him for a fool at Tenby?

Danny recalled Jamie had become known in the weighing room as 'the Bunsen burner'. 'I reckon they're wrong about you.'

'Thanks, I think,' Bunce replied and left with, 'Hope you find your answers, though I'm still unsure what the question is.'

Danny barely noticed he was now alone. He knew changing the bend couldn't happen unless one person was fully on board – the clerk of the course, Sophie Towers.

Danny left the saddling box too, aware a runner in the next race would soon arrive.

He always suspected amateur stewards, jockeys, and trainers were all open to corruption but hadn't reckoned upon the clerks of the courses.

'I'm sorry,' read the text. It seemed Sophie had a lot more to apologise for than that image sent to Meg's phone.

In anger Danny had replied with a threat to end her career. Yet she brushed it off by implying she wouldn't need to work again. That would certainly be true if she was part of the White Turf Group selling land on to developers.

Danny had ruled her out as a means to push the Ely sale through as she didn't have a vote, but she sat in on every board meeting and was a respected voice that could sway the members.

He reckoned she'd only sent the email with the photo attachment to distract him from discovering the truth behind any corrupt practices going on at her racetrack.

He caught the next train back to Ely platform. He had to get there before Sophie locked up for the final time.

As he sat there in the window seat on the return to Ely station, Shropshire and Monmouthshire was just a blur of green to Danny as they cut through the countryside. He was even oblivious to the tinny heavy metal from the long-haired teen's headphones in the seat opposite.

About to return the drone image to the knee pocket of his combats, he caught a glimpse of the list of figures on the back. He knew the clerk of the course couldn't slow down the pace to a race without bribing every jockey lining up and even then, the handicapper would see from video of the race that it had been falsely run.

That left the distance and going of the race as potential tools to manipulate the time clocked. If the two horseshoe rings scribbled by Howard related to the distance the horses were covering on the bend the only other factor under the clerk's control was the going of the turf. He studied the two columns of figures. Danny could see them differently now, like they'd suddenly been translated for him. They had to be readings from the going stick.

He knew the reading on the going stick range from zero for a quagmire and fifteen for tarmac at the other extreme.

The right column on the back of the drone image had consistently higher figures.

To weaken the form of certain races they'd need to declare the ground as firmer than it actually was. That would undermine the time clocked for the race as generally the harder the ground the quicker it is for a horse to get from start to finish.

The right column must therefore show the declared going readings for each Ely meeting. He guessed the lower numbers in the left column must've been Howard's assessment of the actual going at these meeting.

But these going readings were an average from around the complete circuit of Ely Park and they were fed into the brain of the going stick before being sent to the media and authorities. How the hell could they corrupt them at will?

Had she over- or under-watered with the sprinklers at different meetings to create fake ground?

Racegoers in the stands and hacks up in the press box would surely ask questions if she wasn't switching on the sprinkler system when the ground was already firm.

Howard had sketched the rings to show how they were changing the distance. Shame he hadn't done the same for the going readings, not just a list of numbers. He could see what was happening but didn't know how Sophie Towers had done it.

All his life he'd found it hard to trust people, let them into his life. Over time he'd allowed Sophie to be an exception. He felt comfortable around her. Now he felt betrayed, a fool.

Danny slipped the photo away and shut his eyes, trying to push back the anger simmering inside. He didn't want to do something he'd later regret when he got there.

CHAPTER 17

Danny tracked the well-trod path towards Sophie's office high up in the doomed Ely Park grandstand.

He glanced across at the aircraft hangar of a store barn. It made his look like a potting shed. He stopped on the path to look closer. The barn door was open. Like back at the yard, he reckoned only a select few among the Ely ground staff would be allowed keys, namely the clerk of the course.

Danny ducked under the rail and quickened his stride towards the open door, eager to catch Sophie before she vanished.

As he neared, he noticed a yellow skip outside, clearly to get rid of whatever couldn't be flogged at auction.

Danny was about to enter the opening when he heard a loud bang bounce off the walls inside.

He froze. He turned to the skip in search of something sharp to defend himself. Inside the container, it was mostly a tangle of broken plastic railing and posts, and seats torn from the stands.

Among the junk, he saw something shiny and new.

Danny fished it out. A Tracktion 2.3 going stick.

He swore Sophie reckoned it was worth over a grand. He was surprised it was with this crap and had not found a buyer.

Perfect, he thought, about to test the spiked end as a potential weapon.

He was left disappointed. The tapered file had been damaged with the end bent over like a hook. He looked harder. This wasn't by accident. The hook had been shaped.

Minutes after the Ely fall, he recalled Sophie demonstrate the going stick. At the time he was just about lucid enough to recall her pulling the going stick out of the ground at a forty-five degree angle to measure the traction felt by a horse's hoof leaving the ground. The more effort it took, the harder the ground. Danny's fingertips touched the bent end. That would make it a lot tougher to pull out. They must've switched the regular going stick with this one when they needed a faster ground reading to devalue the form of selected races some more.

162

To Danny, he could see it had more worth as evidence than a weapon.

He hid the going stick behind the skip for now. He heard another crashing bang inside. He crept to the black of the door mouth. From there he could make out an indistinct female voice chattering away.

She really has gone insane, Danny thought, as he activated his phone's torch and splashed some light in there.

He saw Sophie Towers standing holding a bundle of plastic sections of railing.

'Destroying the evidence I see,' Danny said. 'You missed one over there.'

She dropped them on a pile presumably ready for that skip.

'I don't blame you,' he added, 'best to shift the hot goods before someone turns up and works out how you cheated the handicap system.'

She stopped breathing hard. 'How much do you know?'

'Everything,' he replied. His eyes homed in on her right hand as it felt the pocket of her grey jogging top.

As she brushed by heading for the exit, Danny edged into her path.

'Too late for any of that,' she said and winked. 'You had your chance in the tent.'

When she reached the gap of light, Danny called after her, 'Aren't you forgetting something?'

Danny waggled her mobile in his hand as she turned.

'Give it back.'

'Just teaching you a life-lesson,' he said. 'Never pat where your valuables are, might as well hand them to a pickpocket.'

'Hand it over, Danny!'

Instead, he switched the phone on. 'Let's see what we've got here.'

He opened the internet browser hoping to see she'd kept logged into some of Gash's numerous betting accounts. But instead there were just two webpages open.

The first showed a printable boarding pass for a non-stop flight bound from Bristol to Geneva departing this evening.

'Going on holiday, nice,' Danny said.

She scowled as said replied, 'I've been working hard. The break will do me good.'

'I bet it will,' Danny said. 'Good enough to stay there permanently. Lucky you've only booked a one-way ticket.'

Danny checked the other page. It was a guest pass for the meeting that featured the Grand Prix de St Moritz on Sunday week.

'Off to the races,' he added, 'another busman's holiday?'

'Give it here!'

'I hope you see a *flying machine* over there,' Danny said recalling the entry made by the owners White Turf Group.

Her eyes widened. 'It seems you really do know everything.'

'You reshaped the bends, at night I guess, when no one else could see,' Danny said.

'First to arrive, last to leave,' she said. 'Like you say, I'm a grafter. They're light and interconnect with ease, child's play.'

'By increasing the distance of the bend and making the ground firmer than advertised, you were creating an illusion that the runners were slow plodders that deserved a low rating and therefore a low weight to carry in a handicap next time out and no one else would ever know.'

'But this couldn't happen at every meeting,' she said. 'As the standard or average times for each distance used by form students as a guide to assess the time clocked would eventually readjust upwards, our fake slower times would effectively become the norm.' She sighed. 'All good things must come to pass I guess, and it's time now to cash in while I'm ahead.'

'You had to trust that the placer of the bets, Gash, wouldn't get some of his own cash on at the best price before you,' Danny asked.

'He came highly recommended by you, remember?'

Danny shook his head.

'At the Ely Park Christmas do you told me his name and where you'd last seen him, so a belated "thank you" is in order,' she said. 'Without you, perhaps all this wouldn't have happened.'

'You can't pin this on me.' Danny would have admired the scam had it not resulted in this place shutting and many thousands of punters being duped. 'Was it always your plan?'

'For what?'

'Build this place up then tear it down,' Danny said.

She sighed.

'Don't be ashamed, it's the perfect crime make a bundle by swindling the other punters and then make an even bigger bundle destroying all evidence. What puzzles me is how you convinced all of the parties involved in the decision to sell a track riding high.'

'That was the easy part,' she said, seemingly revelling in this opportunity to show off. 'The BHA were desperate to keep any scandal that might harm the sport's reputation from going public, the councillors in town planning were desperate for flat land near the city and the Ely board members were desperate to pocket a massive dividend for their share in the track. And there isn't a thing you can do to stop it now.'

Danny chucked over her phone. He knew there'd have been be no point smashing the screen as she'd only have downloaded the tickets again.

'Why send that selfie to Meg?'

'I wanted to drive a wedge in your marriage.'

He now knew why she was a confirmed singleton and would probably end up a spinster. He could no longer see her obvious beauty on the outside.

'Well that's one thing you've done that didn't work.'

'It did work as it distracted you for a while, that was the intention. I knew you'd have enough on your plate at home to worry about what was going on here, ambassador or no ambassador,' she said and then stopped to think. 'And here's something else for you to regret, I'd have gone all the way if you'd wanted, always had a thing for you, Danny.'

'No regrets from me,' Danny said. 'I suppose you sent Gash to try the same with Meg.'

'He was sent there to find out what you'd been told by Howard at Doncaster,' she said. 'He surpassed himself when I heard he'd made a play for Meg.' She paused. 'You know, I'll miss this place, I'll miss you.' She quickly wiped her eyes. 'Bloody dust.'

Danny saw something just then that made him believe at least a small part of her had yet to be infected by greed. There was a human being. He was convinced he saw some regret, sorrow. A return of the old Sophie Towers he'd got to know, trust. Perhaps he just wanted to see it, a trick of the light.

He waited for Sophie to be gone for good. He then left there for the last time and couldn't get home quick enough. Oddly, getting to know Sophie better had made him appreciate and love Meg all the more. When he got back she'd left a note on the lounge table saying she was out on a hack.

Danny went to his office to wait for her return. As he sat there he couldn't figure out how to get back at Sophie. He couldn't just turn up at St Moritz on spec, hoping there'd be ticket touts or a spare one due to a last minute cancellation.

He looked up at the wall and saw his trainer's licence, framed and behind glass.

That's it! The answer was right in front of him.

He returned to the entry page for the race-card featuring the Grand Prix to St Moritz. This time it wasn't the big race that interested him. He checked the supporting card and his heart started to pump when he saw there was a maiden for three-year-olds as an aperitif to the big race half an hour before.

He knew the only two horses kept on the boil since the illness ravaged the yard were Zebrawood and Pobble Beach, both turned three on 1st January like the rest of the fourteen thousand horses in training.

Danny knew he had to choose which one he should enter to get a pass into the track.

His heart said Garrick Morris's Zebrawood, who could also represent a pass to even greater riches, or Pobble Beach, who he now knew won an Ely maiden in a much better adjusted time than was printed in the formbook.

Deep down, he knew there was no choice. Pobble Beach had proved a class apart when blowing away Zebrawood on the gallops and was the only one worthy of representing his yard on the world stage.

He registered with the Swiss Jockey Club, and then booked the chestnut colt into the race on Sunday.

He knew there'd be a jittery week ahead, hoping the forensic lab hadn't discovered any of his DNA at Howard's place.

A sudden knock at his office door made him jump. He stood as fight or flight impulses kicked in.

166

The door slowly opened. A sweaty face appeared in the crack.

'Meg! I didn't hear you come back,' he said.

'I didn't hear you either,' she said.

'Good workout?'

'For me more than the horse,' she said, wiping sweat from her pink cheeks. 'Aren't you going to ask why the police called?'

'I was afraid of the answer.'

'What have you done to be afraid?'

'Nothing,' Danny said, 'you know I have a problem with the police, whether I've done something or not.'

'But you ran away again,' she said. 'Luckily, all their questions were for me.'

'Really?'

Meg nodded as she came over and leant on the desk. 'I told Beth about that slime ball Gash, and she only went and reported it on my behalf.'

'And that's the only reason they came flashing their blue lights.'

She nodded. 'See? You needn't have to run. You're way too uptight sometimes, Danny.' She rested her cold hands on his tight shoulders and started to knead them. 'I've missed you.'

He recalled Sophie say the same but hearing the words actually meant something this time. It felt good.

Danny casually closed the lid of the laptop showing the Swiss entry form. This wasn't the best time to reveal he was planning on going away again.

'I didn't interrupt anything did I?' she asked.

'Nothing that can't wait,' Danny said.

'It's just, I think I need a long, hot shower,' she said, 'you could join me if you like?'

Danny smiled and took her hand. A shower had never sounded so tempting.

CHAPTER 18

Danny arrived at St Moritz in plenty of time for the racing, enough to walk a circuit of the massive frozen lake overlooked by pretty chalets and ski lodges.

He'd planned to inspect the bends and straights of compacted snow on thick ice, though the surroundings at this famous ski resort had proved distracting.

Sitting in the shadow of the towering snow-topped Alps and the frosted alpine forests clinging to its foothills below, this most seasonal of racetracks was like nothing he'd ever seen before.

He had thought Cleeve Hill overlooking Cheltenham was the most stunning backdrop for a racetrack until now.

Although serene and beautiful, it made his stomach tighten. He preferred familiarity. This would be a stride into the unknown for both jockey and horse.

Unbeaten colt Pobble Beach had taken the flight well and had eaten up in the warmth of the indoor American-style barn housing the competitors on the lake.

Danny had felt reluctant to leave him there. He had become protective of the berated chestnut, perhaps because he was now the yard's best prospect, along with Doncaster hero Gunslinger, among the flat racers.

Checking the schedule, thoroughbreds weren't the only stars of this show. Also competing were Standardbreds, Arabian horses, and skijoring – where horses were trained to pull riders on skis.

Danny always felt safer sitting on the horse than being behind one. This already felt like enough of a departure from the norm.

Neither of their preparations had been ideal; Pobble Beach had slipped on the Ely bend when last seen and Danny had never even worked a horse on snow.

He knew the local jockeys and horses would have more than an edge round here.

Pobble Beach was now being shod with snow-rim pads on each foot – lined with a tube to pop out any snow or ice balls collecting in the hoof – by experienced local farriers.

That gave Danny some time to explore several white-pitched tents selling everything from hot food to luxury goods, like designer watches and jewellery. Many didn't have price tags which made Danny think twice about asking. In any case, he wasn't there for the shopping. He was after Sophie Towers.

Mingling, he rubbed shoulders with a mix of racegoers and socialites wrapped in furs, ski jackets, hats and scarves, some accompanied by dogs.

This playground for the rich and famous was a place to see and be seen. Danny felt as aware of himself as they appeared to be. He didn't fit in at all.

He began to wonder if any of them were members of Sophie's publicity-shy consortium known only as the White Turf Group. There was no way of knowing until he saw them gather as owners of the four-year-old Flying Machine in the parade ring before the feature Grand Prix de St Moritz.

After a while he began to pick up on the festive atmosphere as he heard a saxophone playing off in the distance while he gazed at a towering sculpture of a Trojan Horse that had been rolled on to the ice.

He glanced over at a sign on the racetrack that read: White Turf St Moritz. The finish line.

On the infield beyond, he spotted a black-and-white hand-operated scoreboard, like he'd seen on racetracks and by village cricket pitches years back. It was already showing the horses names and numbers for the opener. Perhaps the electronics would freeze up here.

Sophie was still nowhere to be seen. Maybe she'd already seen him and was gone.

He was glad of the body protector under his silks and jacket, for warmth as much as protection yet he still shivered. The race time was nearing.

Better go check on the future star of Silver Belle Stables, he thought. He returned to the barn and tacked up the colt.

He was confident the memory of the Ely slip hadn't left its mark mentally. He'd got up quick enough and hadn't turned a hair since.

'Made of sterner stuff, boy, aren't you?' he whispered into the large ears as he led the unbeaten three-year-old out into the

169

parade area behind the tents. 'Sophie made sure you were undervalued. I won't do the same. I want the world to show how good you really are.'

Cantering Pobble Beach to the start on the home straight, Danny was glad he'd been handed tinted goggles. The glare was like an interrogation lamp as the crisp, pure white snow dazzled in the winter sun. He could see why the rails were painted blue with yellow posts to stand out as a guide on this one-lap tour of the lake.

The thin, frosty air stung his exposed face and lungs. He pulled up the woollen neck muffler over his red nose and measured his breaths. Now was not the time to panic, he thought, the inexperienced colt would only pick up on it.

The green stalls were lighter and wirier than the standard British equivalent. He hoped Pobble Beach would adapt as well as he had to the alien surroundings. It was still the same pre-race prep: load up, wait, and then react to the springs of the paddle doors.

They'd loaded up fine. Pobble Beach was looking about, probably curious why the landscape had suddenly turned white having been in the Valleys just hours earlier.

Up ahead Danny saw a flagman dressed in green with matching flag step out on to the track a couple of furlongs away, near the start of the first sharp right turn.

Danny suddenly forgot how to breathe. He forced air down into his lungs, chilling his windpipe and feeding his racing heart.

Suddenly the crowds hushed in both seated stands lining the home stretch to their left.

Danny gripped the reins tighter.

This has nothing on the Pardubice and Grand National fences, he thought, desperately trying to boost his shrivelling confidence. He still knew coming down on solid ice would hurt far more than rain-softened turf.

He simply didn't know how hard to take on the first bend. He wanted to let others take the lead and learn from them, though he knew his horse relished trailblazing when landing the Ely maiden.

Suddenly, the grilles vanished and instinct took over.

Danny pushed with all his strength. He wanted to get ahead of the rivals and a snowstorm of kickback. However, he soon realised this wasn't a revolutionary idea as the local jockeys seemingly had the same plan of attack.

Pobble Beach couldn't go with this thunderous early dash and he wasn't going to get drawn into forcing a breakneck pace.

Instead, he eased back, tucking in behind the two early leaders, among them being the German-trained favourite Seascape.

Danny fought off the urge to shut his eyes as he was pelted with snowballs and splinters of flying ice from out of the white powdery clouds kicked up by the hurtling half-ton thoroughbreds.

Two furlongs in, the fearless Pobble Beach attacked the first bend when Danny wanted to take it steady. The headstrong colt won the argument, surefootedly banking right. Suddenly, he was back swinging on the bridle, as if growing in confidence with every raking stride.

Danny made sure to stay on the outer in his rippling green and brown silks, three horse-widths off the yellow and blue of the rail.

Just over a furlong later and the field of eight had straightened to face the short backstretch.

Danny fed off his charge's exuberance. It was infectious. He felt there was still plenty of horse under him and saw his chance to make a decisive move. He sat lower and urged his colt to go by the leaders. He felt the strong youngster lengthen his stride and fill his lungs, quickening willingly.

Soon they'd drawn alongside and then headed the favourite Seascape, with the other joint leader already beginning to backpedal.

Danny pushed harder as he wanted to bag the rail before the second bend. In his obsessive mind, this became a race within a race.

Now front-rank, it felt like they'd escaped from a huge snow fight.

He could sense Pobble Beach was loving this. Danny, less so. He'd seen another sharp right looming large.

He glanced over at local hero Gabriel Muller, whose focus sensibly lay firmly ahead. It was too late to ask for any hints or tips.

Running out of backstretch Danny gave up any notion of overtaking the favourite hugging the rail. He settled for matching

171

strides one horse-width wide, feeling it might reduce any loss in momentum by lessening the severity of the turn.

Turning for home, Danny could already hear the cheers from the crowds sat in the two stands lining the home stretch by the TV camera tower, drowning out the rhythmic crunching thud of hooves on the snow.

He suspected most were urging on the local favourite.

Danny knew this was an away match and wasn't deterred as he sat even lower and asked Pobble Beach to stretch those athletic chestnut legs on the sprint for home.

Muller was alive to the move on Seascape and edged ahead. Danny overcame the snow blindness to catch a flash of the big screen on the white infield.

'Come on, boy! Prove them wrong,' he growled.

Pobble Beach suddenly found extra, eager to please his master.

Danny couldn't now disappoint the brightest pupil among his current crop of Flat racers.

He wanted this as much for the horse as for him. Perhaps this was the highlight he could take from an otherwise wretched winter.

'More,' Danny shouted. 'More!'

As they flashed by the winning post, Danny extended his arms to stretch Pobble Beach's long chestnut neck where it mattered most, head down by the sign he'd seen on the winning post.

Crossing the finish line, he had no clue who had won. He could, however, tell from the excited German commentary that it was close.

Danny gathered the reins to slow Pobble Beach, who appeared ready to go round again.

As they walked back to the parade area round the back, he nervously awaited the result of the photo.

Suddenly the speakers came to life. '*Erste Nummer funf,* Pobble Beach.'

Danny was the only one to punch the air.

For a blissful moment, he forgot all his worries as he'd ridden and owned his first winner since that fateful day at

Doncaster. Blood spiked with adrenalin, he felt like he could've scaled the mountainside nearby.

Danny led the youngster in. He only hoped those TV cameras had beamed these pictures back to Meg on a racing channel in the UK.

He collected the trophy, lowering his neck muffler for the photo.

He then hung around and saw connections of the big race start to stream into the pre-parade ring.

He recognised Lucas Schmidt – the trainer of Flying Machine – from an online image search. The men in suits around him were less familiar. The publicity-shy consortium had come out to play, Danny thought. Except there was one that seemingly still couldn't face the world, wearing a thick ski jacket with fur-lined hood pulled up.

Sophie Towers, Danny reckoned, finally.

He knew they'd be in there until the bell rang for jockeys to mount.

Proudly leading the winner back to the barn, Danny saw a man rushing over from the direction of a flash new restaurant behind the tented village.

Danny hoped it was a rich owner looking to invest after seeing him win.

The man was buttoned into a waistcoat with just a beard to warm his fat face. As he neared, Danny saw he was right about the rich owner bit.

'All right, Garrick? Small world.'

Was the Welsh billionaire part of the White Turf Group?

'What the hell do you think you're playing at?'

That greeting didn't bode well for any future investment, Danny thought.

'You clearly thought more of this lowly rated maiden winner than the promising blueblood I took the trouble of sending you.'

Danny stopped turning Pobble Beach. This sounded more serious than he'd thought.

'I just thought Pobble Beach would be better suited.'

'I'm entertaining close friends up there,' he said. Danny detected a slur. 'Think how fucking marvellous this would've been

173

for me to show off a winner in my colours. Instead you selfishly profit from one of your own. I don't think you're taking my offer seriously, I don't think you're taking me seriously!'

'It's not that at all, Garrick, it's just Zebrawood hasn't been firing on the gallops like this one.'

'How can he? This … thing won a shitty Ely maiden, mine has been up there at the grade one tracks,' Garrick said, pointing at Pobble Beach. Danny wanted to cover the colt's ears. He took those words personally.

'Give it up, Garrick, you're drunk.'

'I'm sober enough to know you've ruined Zebrawood,' Garrick snapped. 'And he'll be out of your yard before you even think of begging.'

Danny bit his lip but he desperately wanted to speak his mind.

Suddenly he was distracted by the hooded figure in a blue ski jacket he'd seen with the other connections of the White Turf Group's horse Flying Machine in the parade ring.

Danny was about to hand Pobble Beach over to racecourse staff to be fed and watered in the barn when Garrick slurred, 'I haven't finished with us.'

Danny came over to look him in the eye. 'I have.'

He stared at Garrick as he struggled to keep his footing on his way back to the restaurant.

'That's the sight of a multimillion pound investment walking away,' Danny told Pobble Beach, 'and you know what, I'm kind of glad.'

Garrick seemed like he'd be harder work than even he was worth.

He left the colt in safe hands and followed the hooded figure out of the racecourse. He couldn't fathom why an owner with such a high-profile runner could possibly leave before watching the big race.

Danny suspected he was the reason. Sophie had been spooked.

CHAPTER 19

Danny tracked the hooded figure out of the racetrack gates and off the lake.

Sophie wouldn't leave like this when all the other owners had stayed unless something was wrong.

He reckoned she'd seen his face when he'd lowered the neck muffler on the presentation podium.

Danny went after her to find answers.

He kept his eyes fixed on the back wrapped in a blue thickly padded ski jacket, determined not to let her escape as she had from Ely's store barn last week.

His riding boots crunched the impacted snow as they trudged by restaurants and shops selling hiking and skiing equipment.

As they left the town centre and began to climb, the chalets either side of the roads they snaked had become less frequent.

From up there he glanced back down at the lake with the runners for the one-mile four-furlong feature. They were little more than colourful dots as they circled before facing two laps of the lake.

Perhaps Sophie preferred to watch the races alone through high-powered binoculars from high above. Maybe she'd fallen out with the other investors in the consortium.

Danny was panting even harder as they showed no sign of stopping. He had thought the air was thin enough on the lake.

He made sure to keep a good twenty yards between them. Thankfully she had never looked round, not even for that view.

He afforded a glance at the large, snow-laden chalets either side facing downslope towards the lake. He couldn't imagine how anyone could possibly afford them, but something like a betting scam and dodgy real estate deal would do, he reckoned.

Suddenly, his phone buzzed against his aching thigh.

Not now, he thought.

His furtive eyes flicked between the blue back of the hooded owner and the small screen of his phone displaying Stony's number.

Danny slowed to allow the gap to grow. He answered with a strangled whisper. 'Yes?'

'Danny? You got a cold or something.'

'What is it?'

He knew any sound would be amplified in this silent setting shrouded by thick snow.

'Good to hear from you too, Danny,' Stony said as if miffed by Danny's tone. 'Don't know why I bothered really.'

'I can't speak now,' Danny explained.

'Well I can,' Stony replied. 'You see, I remember now.'

'Remember what?'

'Middlesex County Racing Club,' Stony replied. 'I was on my way to the Flutter House, when I realised I was wrong. Kempton wasn't the only track in Middlesex, there was another one.' Danny recalled Howard reveal there'd been over sixteen hundred racecourses, both run under rules and in point-to-points, come and go down the centuries in Britain. 'Showing my age forgetting it. Mind I'd always thought Alexandra Park was in Greater London.'

'Wha—'

'Alexandra Park.'

Alex Park!

'Holy shit,' Danny whispered. Howard's final act was to protect the badge with his fingers. It was his only chance to nail the killer.

Howard had said he'd chosen every badge for a reason. He wasn't kidding.

'Holy shit indeed,' Stony said. 'How the hell did I forget dear old Ally Pally? As a kid, I used to skip school to go there when my dad was based down that way, till it shut its gates in 1970 of course. Over the years top jocks like Scobie Breasley, Lester Piggott and Geoff Lewis regularly rode there. Bloody dangerous, mind, they used to call it the "Frying Pan", some jockeys reckoned its sharp, cambered bends were a potential death trap.'

Suddenly, the hooded figure stopped ahead.

'Gotta go,' Danny mumbled.

'Let me finish my story first, you're the first person I've spoken to today … anyway, one time I recall—'

Danny had to shut his phone down.

He hadn't even fully digested the news when the hooded figure slowly turned. Had they heard his voice?

Danny scanned the area to seek cover.

He didn't have time to reach the Jeep parked up in the nearest driveway.

To his right, there was a bank of deep crisp snow, probably pushed there earlier in the day to clear the road.

He turned away from the bank and fell back, allowing his whole body to be swallowed by the soft snow.

He knew from where the hooded figure had turned he'd be concealed by the snow side on.

Danny lay there perfectly still, staring up at the darkening blue sky, hoping the hooded figure had turned again and carried on the climb.

He was safely shielded side-on, but for how long?

He counted in his head. Eight … nine … ten …

Every second he dreaded seeing the silhouetted shape of Alex's head block out the light above. He suddenly felt very vulnerable lying their unarmed and alone on the mountainside with a suspected serial killer.

Fifteen … sixteen …

Ample time for them to have double-backed here, he reckoned.

He raised his head from the Danny Rawlings-shaped hole he'd made and looked upslope. The hooded figure had gone. He'd been slipped again.

Danny got up as he dusted off the powdery snow and then headed up to the point where he'd seen the figure stop and turn.

From there he could make out three distinct tracks of footprints made since the last snowfall.

From the tread patterns, only one of them was heading upslope. He followed that track for another half mile until the prints turned into the drive of a luxurious Swiss chalet, though it looked big enough to be a ski lodge.

From there the tracks vanished as the driveway had been cleared of snow. Danny wasn't concerned. He was certain he'd arrived.

The pitched roof was covered in a thick smooth layer of fresh snow, like icing on a cake, and exposed beams and ornate carvings decorated the balconies and porch.

There was an inviting yellow glow coming from the downstairs windows above the raised wooden decking out the front. It could make a Christmas card.

Danny's honed skills as a housebreaker kicked in as he crept cat-like to the front door. He crawled to one of the two large front windows, both starting to mist up from the inside.

And there he was. Alex Park. Stony was right.

He was stood there in just a towel wrapped round his waist.

He looked like he was folding his jacket on the kitchen island. Beyond was a spacious lounge area with a wooden staircase to the far side near a massive flat-screen TV on the wall showing racing from the lake far below.

Similar open-plan living as he'd seen in Penarth, Danny thought, only supersized here.

Alex flexed his pecs and biceps strutting by a mirror hung between two doors on the right.

In better shape than me, Danny was ashamed to admit.

Off to the left Danny could see plumes of steam escaping an open door. It reminded him of the saunas off the changing rooms at some of the bigger tracks for jockeys to shed a few pounds and make the correct weight.

Danny watched Alex disappear into the sweat room. He then waited for the clap of the door shutting.

He got up from his haunches and then waited a few seconds, just in case Alex had forgotten to take something to read in with him.

He turned the handle of the heavy wooden door and was surprised to see it swing open. Alex was clearly expecting someone.

Danny rushed in from the cold. He then stepped as quietly as is possible in riding boots on a hardwood floor over to the jacket on the island.

He was looking for some proof that Alex was involved in the betting scam and the killing of Howard Watkins and Larry Wallace, even if it was a just photo of him with Sophie Towers.

From a false inner lining, he felt something cold and metallic.

He pulled out a handgun. He quickly pocketed the bullets, rubbed the handle he'd touched and slid the weapon back where he'd found it.

He was about to search the kitchen for a knife when there was a thud of a fist on the front door. Danny was just glad they hadn't tried the handle.

Would Alex hear that? Would he bother to open it?

He would if he was expecting a visitor.

Danny couldn't risk finding out.

He rushed to the wall facing the sauna on the opposite side.

There was a single and a double door either side of Alex's version of a vanity mirror.

Danny reckoned the double door would be some kind of store cupboard. He opened it. Behind he heard the slap of wet feet from beyond the sauna door.

Danny quickly contorted his body to the shape of a gap between ski-boards, coats, ski poles, hiking boots, rucksacks, ropes and crampons.

He crouched there, eye pressed to the crack of light between the doors.

There was another bang on the door.

Suddenly the door to the sauna room opened, releasing another plume of steam.

Alex emerged naked, except for a towel over his shoulder. Clearly he knew the visitor.

When he opened the door, he reached for the towel. 'Oh, Jesus, it's you.'

Gash came in, glancing down. 'Blimey.'

'It's cold, all right?' Alex said, covering his modesty.

'No wonder you're so angry all the time,' Gash said. 'Who were you expecting?'

'Alton,' Alex replied. 'Now what the hell do you want?'

'What's owing me.'

'I owe you nothing.'

'Ten per cent cut of all profits. That's what we agreed at the start.'

'But I risked the money.'

179

'I risked—'

'Go on, Gash. What the hell did you risk?' Alex growled. He came up closer. Alex's presence more than made up for his height and heft in this match-up.

'Your reputation?' Alex said and sniggered. 'I took you on precisely for being a born loser. And guess what, you've lost again. Still, you should be used to it by now.'

Danny could now understand why Sophie had changed since he'd known her.

'I'm not leaving until I get my share. Fuck, even your Flying Machine won the feature, take it out of that.'

'Spoiler alert,' Alex said, 'I was about to watch a recording.'

Danny was now certain Alex was the mastermind behind the White Turf Group.

'Why aren't you even there?'

'There was someone on track I didn't particularly want to meet,' Alex said. Danny swallowed. 'And now there's one in my chalet too. I'm going to ask politely for you to leave.'

'Or you'll what?' Gash said and shoved Alex away. 'I'm sick of you bossing me. You're a bully.'

'You're a bully,' Alex returned the words in a childish voice. 'I want you gone, before Sophie gets here.'

Danny could see Gash was breathing heavily. There was a silence.

The quiet before the storm, Danny sensed.

'I saw you chatting up some woman at the bar on track,' Gash said. 'I'm sure Sophie would like to know about it. Pay me and I'm gone, forever.'

'Resorting to blackmail now I see,' Alex said and came closer. 'Unfortunately for you, Sophie would believe me over you about anything. The slag's wet for me.'

Alex slapped Gash's flushed cheeks. 'Tell you what, let me get changed first and I'll see what I can do.'

That didn't sound as promising as it ought to, Danny thought.

He sat there perfectly still as he watched Gash idly strum his fingers on the granite kitchen top.

Suddenly, Gash appeared to look directly at him.

Danny quickly removed his face from the slit of light. Gash was coming over.

Danny's heart began to pound against his body protector. He was about to pre-empt the doors flinging open. He tensed his limbs, ready to burst from there.

And then he recalled the full-length mirror between the doors. Gash had come over to inspect himself not the cupboard.

Danny was safe, for now.

The sauna door opened again. Alex had put on a casual navy pullover and black trousers.

'I can take cash, or bank transfer,' Gash said.

Something about Alex's face told Danny he hadn't come out to discuss payment methods.

'You've got some fucking cheek coming here,' Alex said. 'My private chalet.'

'You gave me your address to do the transfers for the winnings.'

'And the winnings were far greater than any of us expected,' Alex said.

'So?'

'You had no part in our success,' Alex said. 'We never agreed performance-related pay.'

'But we did discuss pay,' Gash snapped.

'Ten per cent is way more than you deserve. I mean, I did all the hard work, took all the risk, you just tapped the sodding screen in the bookmaker accounts.'

'We agreed!'

'Really? That's funny, I can't remember any contract.'

'You know full well there's no contract,' Gash said. 'There never is in this line of work, for good reason.'

'Well then, I think I owe you ...' He came up close again and made a zero with his wet finger and thumb.

'This isn't funny,' Gash said. 'I need that money. I've got gambling debts.'

'Oh, the irony,' Alex said.

Gash grabbed Alex by his pullover. 'It was an oral contract we made, you'd better fucking honour it.'

'Or?'

181

'I'll go to the Swiss Guard,' Gash said. 'I'll tell them everything about the betting fraud.'

'They can't prove anything now the rails and the going stick have been destroyed,' Alex explained. 'The crime scene is gone.'

Danny started to get cramp in his toes. He reckoned it was a delayed reaction to the cold. The thin plastic of his riding boots weren't designed for the arctic conditions outside. He fought off the urge to shake his foot. One sound from in there and he was dead.

'You can afford something for me,' Gash pleaded. 'That property deal must've netted millions. Give me some! Give it!'

Gash shook Alex, who wrestled himself free.

Danny then saw Alex start to bounce on his toes like a boxer, as if Gash had inadvertently flicked a switch in Alex's brain.

Alex came for him. First he swiped Gash's legs from under him. Gash fell back, cracking his head on the granite corner of the kitchen island.

Alex flung himself on the bigger man, like a feral animal in for the kill. His hands stretched around Gash's fleshy neck.

Gash started to twitch like a dying fish. And then lay there, still as a corpse.

Danny was about to leap out when he saw the growing moat of blood around Gash's head. He was already dead.

'Oh, Jesus, no, not here,' Alex said, and held his head. 'You fucking idiot.'

Danny wasn't sure whether he was talking to the body bloodying his floor or himself.

Alex went to the kitchen and came back with a canister. There appeared to be a flame symbol on the side.

Lighter fluid, Danny feared, or some other kind of accelerant. Even the canister was supersized compared to the one he had in Penarth.

He heard the sloshing of liquid over wood and could soon smell the heady fumes.

Alex had returned to the steam room and soon emerged with a flaming towel held at arm's reach.

Danny swallowed. This place was about go up like a tinder box.

He must have dipped the towel in the coal fire of the sauna.

Alex's alert brown eyes traced a path to the front door as if planning the most direct escape route once he let the towel go.

Danny watched in horror as the flame fell to the glistening pool on the floor and ignited into an almighty ball of white heat.

Alex backed off and made for the door.

Hearing the lock turn, Danny jumped from the store cupboard while he could.

Suddenly a wall of flames guarded the only door out of there.

Danny turned to a window by the staircase.

He returned to the cupboard and picked out a ski pole.

It'll be triple-fucking-glazed over here, Danny fumed. He began to jab at the glass.

Soon he'd made a growing cobweb of white cracks over the pane.

The warm air began to fill with acrid smoke. Danny pulled up the neck muffler over his mouth and kept slamming the glass with the pointed end of the pole.

He glanced back at Gash's body now consumed by the flames, like he was already on a funeral pyre.

Suddenly a breakthrough as the glass smashed. He set about breaking the second pane when a face appeared in the misted glass.

Sophie Towers!

She started to bang the glass. She seemed just as frantic to get in as he was to get out.

Danny signalled her to get out of the way of any broken glass as he broke through the second pane.

As he began to take on the final sheet of glass, he began to choke and splutter from the black air coating his nostrils, windpipe and lungs.

He ducked low and breathed in a lungful of cleaner air down there. He then stood and raised the ski pole behind his head and then javelined the pole through the glass.

Danny could barely see or breathe as he pulled down the sleeve of his jacket. He then punched out the jagged shark's teeth of glass from the window frame.

He stepped back and pictured the hole he'd made, big enough to dive through.

The searing heat from the spreading flames began to burn his cheeks and singe his jacket. It was like a wildfire in there.

He charged forward, trusting his aim, as he dived through the gap he'd made in the glass.

He was struck by a front of ice cold air as he flew from the blazing chalet. He landed ugly but was pillowed by the soft snow on this sheltered side. He quickly shot to his feet, ready to take on Sophie.

He saw her head was lost in the black smoke billowing from the hole he'd made.

'Get back from there!' Danny said and yanked her away from the toxic fumes.

'Where's Alex?! He's in there! I know it!' she cried, trying to break free from Danny's grip.

'Are you kidding?' Danny asked. 'He started it.'

'He wouldn't,' she shrieked. 'It's his place!'

'He had his reasons,' Danny said, 'cremating Gash for one.'

He then bent double in a coughing fit.

'What?'

Danny spat black phlegm on to the snow. 'Your boyfriend killed for a third time.'

'Liar!' Sophie screamed.

Danny knelt and scooped some snow up to wash the black smoke stains from his cheeks and beneath his nostrils.

He heard sirens growing louder.

Danny grabbed her and pulled her close before she lost it completely.

She pushed him away, only to see he was now looking at her mobile.

'Stop doing that!' she cried.

'Start putting it in a different pocket then,' Danny said. 'Come with me.'

Danny found a dark place, away from the flashing lights of the fire brigade now on the scene.

'What are you doing?' Sophie asked.

'Arranging a date for you,' Danny replied.

'Alex is alive?'

Danny nodded as he composed a text.

'Oh, thank god.'

'You won't be saying that when you hear about what he'd been up to.'

'We're spending the rest of our lives together out here,' she said, showing off her diamond encrusted wedding finger to him.

Danny could see the stone and the band were a lot larger than Beth's engagement ring.

'Your hubby-to-be killed Gash.'

'He told me you were trouble.'

'That's a compliment coming from him.'

'You've got Alex wrong.'

'I've just seen him strangle Gash,' Danny said. 'That fire was to destroy evidence. That's a trend with him.'

'He's no killer. I know he's a gentle soul.'

'Then you don't know him at all,' Danny said. 'This isn't the first time. He killed Larry and Howard, poor sods. And all to keep your good thing going. Don't blame yourself for not seeing it, you fell for him. In a way, we all did, apart from Howard and even that was too late.'

'You're wrong, you have to be wrong!'

'You must've known,' he said. 'Alex had just come back from killing his workmate on the fourteenth. There must've been signs he was acting oddly.'

'I do remember that morning, he ordered me out. He seemed ... distant, said a friend had died.'

'Bit economical with the truth,' Danny said.

'He said he'd got some important business and I shouldn't think about returning within the hour. It didn't sound like trouble. He was relaxed. He even asked me about the tennis match I was watching in the lounge and told me to leave the pasta simmering.'

'He was covering his own back,' Danny said. 'He wanted to make it look like he'd been there all afternoon, rather than sticking the knife into Howard just hours earlier. I came to him for an alibi when it turns out he needed one just as bad.'

'I ... I didn't know,' she said. She wiped her eyes.

Her phone buzzed in his hand. Danny read the message. 'He's bitten.'

'You want me to meet him?'

Danny glanced back at the police cars cordoning off the area around the chalet.

He shook his head. 'I'll take over from here.'

CHAPTER 20

'Tell me when,' Danny said.

'He's back at his seat,' the armed Swiss Guard replied, nodding. 'You're safe to go now.'

Danny emerged from a holding room for early arrivals to the restaurant and weaved between full tables of men in tailored suits and women in designer dresses and sparkling jewellery. They all looked at ease in this glitzy new restaurant overlooking a white racetrack now glowing ethereally under the floodlights.

Alex was sat at a two-seater by the window. He was tapping his phone's screen when he said, 'Bottle of your most expensive, and make it quick, I'm expecting someone.'

'She couldn't come,' Danny said.

Alex dropped the phone on the table as he looked up as if he'd seen a ghost.

'What have you done with her?' Alex asked.

'Told her what you're really like,' Danny said, 'seems she changed her mind about you.'

'I'm done with that bitch, anyway. Gives me a chance to sample the local delicacies. The women over here like the finer things in life, finer things that I can now afford. A classier kind of lady. All Sophie wanted was to curl up on the sofa with me, a bowl of chocolate gateaux and an episode of Doc Martin.'

He groaned seemingly just at the thought, like he'd just trod in dog shit.

Danny slipped his jacket off and placed it over a small LCD unit fixed to the table by the glass, allowing wagers to be placed by diners without them having to interrupt the meal.

'That seat's still taken.'

'I'll be your date tonight, shame to waste that expensive plonk.' Danny smiled. 'Do you come here often?'

'What is this?'

'You're surprised I came all this way to Switzerland to find you,' Danny said.

'I'm surprised you're still alive,' Alex replied, 'and not a charred corpse by now.'

Danny paused. 'You knew I was in there?'

Alex nodded. 'Why do you think I'd set my chalet on fire and then locked up?'

'To cover up Gash's murder, perhaps?'

'He was already a ghost. He'd planned to buy a new name, new passport and a new life, he was escaping gambling debts,' Alex said. 'A liability all round.'

'You surely could've cut him ten per cent.'

'Lose a chunk of my hard earnings for him to just blow it all again on a gambling binge?' Alex asked. 'Nah, he had to go, wish I'd done the same to you back in Penarth.'

'Why didn't you?'

'Partly because you were destroying my evidence,' Alex said.

'Your evidence?'

'I had already placed my clothes covered in Howard's blood in that incinerator, not the twigs I'd told you. I had been waiting for night so the smoke would be lost in the dark. By insisting on adding lighter fuel, you were helping me to get rid of it quicker.'

'Another deception, just like your scam.'

'It wasn't a scam, I just knew the system better than most and how to exploit it,' Alex said. 'It's not much different to trainers running their horses over the wrong distance in maidens to disguise their true ability with the aim of getting a low rating for handicaps.'

'But punters can see that in the form book and make a judgement,' Danny replied. 'Your massaging of the form book was hidden from punters. They don't stand a chance as some of the horse's ability is disguised with fake form.'

He slapped the betting slip on the table. 'Not all punters.'

Danny looked at the betting ticket for five thousand Swiss francs on Pobble Beach at four point six to one.

'Shame it couldn't have been for more,' Alex said. 'But the pool system out here means the more you put on, the more you dominate the betting market and the shorter odds you'll get. Prefer the fixed odds me.'

'Just because you and Sophie were the only ones in on it,' Danny said. 'You could snap up the best odds.'

'I always say if there's one thing better than inside info, it's exclusive inside info.' He paused. 'Don't look so glum 'cos you'd inadvertently made me money from winning out there,' Alex said and picked up the pay-out slip. 'This was the other reason I spared you for this long, I'd been waiting for you to run Pobble Beach in a handicap. That horse was a bigger hero to you than you'll even imagine.'

'It really is all about the money with you isn't it.'

'I lost it all overnight as a trader in the City during the crash of 2007,' Alex explained. 'I was dining out in some swanky restaurant like this one evening, lodging with my parents the next. I vowed then I'd get my fortune back. When I saw a vacancy for a handicapper advertised, I reckoned my skill with figures and assessing risk would help. Turns out it did.'

'But a good salary with benefits wasn't enough for you.'

'I'd be dribbling into my soup in a care home by the time I'd made back what I'd lost as a trader.'

'So you saw the vulnerability in the handicapping system.'

'I knew I couldn't do it alone.'

'That's when you roped the love-blind Sophie Towers into doing whatever you needed.'

'We met at a VIP do last year,' he said. 'She was flattered by the attention from someone nearer her age. At first, she seemed happy just being a clerk of the course. But when I convinced her we had a future together, she soon came round to my grander way of thinking.'

'You used her as a means to alter the track's dimensions, including depth.'

'She held all the power there, and all the keys,' he said. 'When I could see the standard times for each distance begin to adjust, I knew it was time to abort. I knew the board of directors would be like putty in her hands – they were all men. She had no trouble convincing them this was the right way forward. I mean, why would Sophie lie to them, she had nothing to gain from recommending the sale of a track that made her a living.'

Danny sighed. He wanted to smash the water jug on the table over Alex's smug face but he knew detectives and uniformed police that had come from the fire scene were discretely looking on.

He had noticed the chattering and clinking of cutlery and glasses had died somewhat. The waiters must've been ordering the other diners to quietly leave. Alex seemed too wrapped up in himself to notice.

Danny knew it would soon kick off. He needed Alex to give him more. 'You admit to killing Howard and Larry.'

'They had it coming,' Alex said, leaning in closer. 'They knew too much. Howard was a nice guy but he didn't know when to shut up. I saw him talking with Larry at Ludlow. He'd gone there to warn him about me.'

'But Howard didn't know it was you behind the gambles back then.'

'It hurt me as much as Larry when I stabbed him.'

'Are you sure about that?' Danny asked.

'I didn't want to do it, but I knew I had to.'

'He died because of your paranoia.'

'I watched him from a dark corner in the onsite bar at Ludlow after racing, wearing a cap with my head down. I slipped a sedative in his drink when he went to the loo. He wasn't surefooted as he left for a fag break. I didn't know whether that was the drink or the drugs. I followed him out and saw he'd found a sheltered spot to light up. I saw my chance and stabbed him. He was making a right mess, it seemed like the fat bastard was bloated with blood, even coughing the stuff up. I had to move him. I needed to get far enough away before Larry's body was found, so I dragged the dead weight to the one place I couldn't see a CCTV looking down.'

'The public phone box.'

'It was a good place, I mean come on, no one uses them now,' he said. 'Apparently he was found by a security guard doing one last sweep before locking up,' Alex said. 'That didn't matter, I was gone by then.'

'You might not have wanted to kill Larry, but you did it,' Danny said. 'And you didn't learn from it either.'

'Howard simply wouldn't let it go,' he said. 'Clive let me in on their plan to keep Case Twelve open, thinking I was a trusted member of the team. Howard rang me that morning. I knew something was up when his voice was shaking and stuttering. He'd worked it all out; Sophie moving the rails and using the tampered going stick, and that I was betting to reap the rewards. Turns out he

190

was too clever for his own good,' Alex said and sipped some water. 'Except for the fact he should've waited for Clive to arrive first to share the information and not shout me down for bringing racing into disrepute. After I hung up, I headed straight for Somerset to scare Howard into silence, convince him to explain to Clive it had been a false alarm and he didn't actually know the mastermind behind it all.'

'But he wasn't scared that easily,' Danny said.

'He put up a struggle. I can see how he'd dragged you into the Doncaster foyer. But I'd got in the first blow as his back was turned,' he said. 'He seemed groggy that morning, like he'd got a migraine or banged his head or something.'

Keen to move Alex on, Danny said, 'What then?'

'I knew Clive would arrive any minute,' Alex said. 'So I left the front door unlocked for him to go in. It seems he just knocked both the front and back doors before leaving.'

'You were the one who cleared out the secret room.'

Alex nodded. 'Howard had shown me the false wall the only previous time I'd been invited there. You can see why I couldn't trust him with keeping a secret.'

Danny carefully removed his coat from over the table not to touch any buttons around the lit screen of the betting terminal.

'Where are you going?' Alex asked.

'Home.'

'What?'

'I've heard enough,' Danny said. 'You see that lit screen. It means the betting terminal is still live. It's recorded every word of your confession.'

'Bullshit,' Alex said. 'Racing finished hours ago.' He looked out at the floodlit lake. 'And there's no Night Turf this evening, the betting operators will be long gone.'

'It's not betting operators on the other end,' Danny said.

'Who is it then?'

'Look behind,' Danny said.

'I'm not falling for that.'

'Have a look in that mirror then,' Danny said. 'Say hello to the Swiss Guard, they've come for you. It's over.'

Danny noticed Alex's hand had disappeared below the table. His arm was straight, as if reaching down to pull something from the pocket of his jacket hung from the chair.

'You bastard!' Alex said. For the first time, he looked around the room. He raised his hand from beneath the table.

Suddenly Danny was looking down the barrel of a handgun.

'Go on, then,' Danny challenged.

The gun started to shake.

'Didn't think so.'

Click. Click. Click.

Alex shook the gun. 'What's wrong with it?'

Click.

'You lost something?' Danny asked, holding up a bullet he'd pulled from his pocket. 'I didn't tell them about the gun as I wanted them to see what you were capable of.'

Alex stretched for a steak knife on the table and then lunged forward. Danny deftly turned and grabbed Alex's wrist.

He had the strength to squeeze the knife to drop on the table. Danny then slammed the hand down and pinned it there as he swiped the knife from the table.

'How the hell did you know it was me?'

'Howard was still alive when you left,' Danny said. 'His final act was to namecheck you with the members badge for Alexandra Park,' Danny said. 'It seems he was too clever for your good too.'

The armed police came rushing into the restaurant. They forced Alex's face flat to the table and pulled his arms behind his back.

'This is non-admissible. I was lured here by that bitch. Where is she? I'll fucking kill her.'

'Tell that to the jury,' Danny said as he was shepherded away to get medical attention for smoke inhalation before filling in his version of events at the station.

CHAPTER 21

Danny sat in his office. He picked up the copy of *The Racing Life* with the headline: *Beach Racing at Tenby Granted Licence*. The strapline below a photo of the South Beach read: *Surprise Announcement Softens Ely Park Blow.*

Seems the BHA have tried to bury the bad news too, Danny thought. Seeing the arrest of handicapper Alex Park was pushed to page four.

Beneath the newspaper had been an envelope he'd put off opening as the return address was High Holborn. Danny was convinced he'd be summoned before a disciplinary panel for somehow bringing the game into disrepute. He began to wonder what sort of penalty or ban he'd get.

Sod it, Danny thought, can't be any worse than that fire.

He ripped it open and read, *Dear Mr Rawlings.*

Okay so far, he thought.

'As part of an ongoing internal review of the procedures and practices of the British Horseracing Authority, we invite you to discuss an opportunity to join our team in the ongoing fight to keep our sport clean.'

Was this some kind of trick or prank?

The watermark on the thick paper appeared genuine, as did the signature.

If this was a prank, it'd have to rank as one of the dullest in history, he reasoned.

Opportunity?

Team?

Danny was as intrigued by the letter as he was suspicious.

He dialled the direct number.

'BHA Chairman Sir Jacob Rice speaking,' came down the line.

'It's Danny Rawlings. I'm holding your letter.'

'I've been expecting your call.'

'What's this about?'

'Due to a recent reshuffle an investigative role in our integrity department has arisen.'

'What's in it for me?'

'Pay will be performance-based but there's a pension plus medical plan. We'll even give you free board at one of the houses on Jockey Club land.'

'Why pick me out?'

'Danny, if Case Twelve had been made public, or left to fester, punter confidence will have been eroded. They have to believe what they are seeing both on the racetrack and in the formbook are real. If punters lose faith in the Clerks of the Course, there isn't a racecourse in the land that won't be affected. We owe you our gratitude.'

Danny recalled being told of the rapid downfall of the Tenby track after the Oyster Maid Coup.

'We must cut these cancers from our sport,' he said.

'If that was Case Twelve, I'm guessing there are at least eleven others like it.'

'Where there's money to be made, corruption is never far behind.'

'That sounds like a lot of work.'

Danny feared becoming even more of a stranger to Meg and the kids. He couldn't cope with that. He still missed his father not being around for his best years.

'No more than the life of a trainer I should imagine,' Rice said. 'And you'll be working under our Integrity Department.'

'Under?'

'Is that a problem?'

'I have a problem with authority,' Danny said. 'Is that a problem?'

There was a pause. 'We can arrange for you to work alongside them if you must.' Suddenly, Danny detected a slight strain in that masterly voice.

'I understand. You're a … forthright chap. I can see why you came highly recommended.'

'Recommended?'

'By an un-named source,' Rice said. 'They described you like bad smell that won't go away.'

'Clive Napier.' Danny recalled the head of handicappers say that, at the same time dangling him over the Esplanade in Tenby.

'It seems you're as intuitive as Clive said,' Rice replied.

'And I'm sure we can find a Jockey Club property for you and your family to relocate rent free.'

'I didn't know the Jockey Club owned land in Wales.'

'They don't.'

'I'll have to move to England?'

'We need you on-call nearby for ... emergencies that might crop up,' he said. 'And for that, you'll have to be based in the South-East.'

'This is a lot to take in.' Danny paused. 'I'll have to run it by Meg first.'

'Of course, you have until tomorrow midday.'

'Bloody hell, you don't hang about.'

'We cannot hang about when there are unsolved cases linked to some of the worst in humanity.'

'You're not selling it to me.'

'I'm trying to warn you, don't take this on if you're not comfortable with the idea,' Rice said, 'because the reality will be far tougher. But I'm convinced you'll be good for racing.'

'I'll call you back with the answer as soon as I've made it.'

Danny pushed back in his swivel chair. He could see a worrying amount of his own reflection in the mirror at the back of the trophy cabinet in the corner. Many had to be returned after one year to present to winning connections of the next renewal. The gallery of framed photos of past successes for the yard were now gathering dust. Perhaps it was time for a change.

Danny heard Meg playfully growl and roar on the landing.

'Daddy! Daddy!' Jack squealed as he bustled into the room, closely followed by Meg with arms out to grab him.

'Mammy Meg's a monster!'

'She's not that bad,' Danny said, grinning.

Meg laughed. 'Thanks.'

Jack giggled as Danny squeezed his son like a bagpipe.

'Come on, Jack, leave daddy to his work. You know the rule.'

'It's okay, Meg, he can stay,' Danny said. 'I'm done here.'

'Doesn't look like it,' she said, glancing at the mess of invoices, receipts and letters covering his desk.

Jack jumped off as if already bored and ran across the landing to his room.

'Wish I had half his energy,' Danny said.

'You okay? Seem a bit flat that's all.'

'Yeah, just been thinking.'

'I thought it was the frozen pipes making that noise.'

Danny didn't react to the joke. 'Come, sit here.'

He stood and made way for her to take the seat.

'I'm honoured,' she said and spun on the swivel chair.

Danny leant forward and grabbed the chair's leather arms to anchor her in front of him. 'I have something important to say.'

'Is this to do with why you ran from the police?' she said, frowning, 'because I don't think I want to know the real reason.'

'This is about us,' Danny said.

'I definitely don't want to know,' she said. 'I understand it's been tough with the horses being sick and I've already said I believe you about Sophie's dirty games.'

'Meg, I've been made an offer by the BHA?'

'An offer? What kind of offer?'

'Work for them to help clean up racing.'

'And you'd do that.'

'I guess I want to give something back to the sport that made me all those memories,' Danny said. 'A sport that's made me.'

'Why the hell did they pick you?' she asked.

Danny chuckled. 'You're supposed to be on my side.'

'I didn't mean it like that,' she said. 'It's just you'd think others would be better qualified.'

'They've just seen something in me I guess,' Danny said. 'It's a guaranteed income, with performance-related bonuses and free rent. No more begging our worst owners to cough up.'

'Where?'

Danny was surprised she'd entertained the idea this long. He guessed she too saw the possibility for a fresh start, shorter hours, and less time apart.

'They want us to move nearer London.'

'Us as in us.'

'All of us, a new start, a challenge,' he replied. 'No more blurry-eyed mornings, no more arguing over silly things.'

'What will I do while you're on a case?'

'Ride out at yards, set up a dance school, whatever it takes to see that smile back.'

'But what about this place, the horses!'

'We can lease it out,' Danny said. 'Pick the most suitable from a shortlist that apply.'

'You'll be lucky to get a shortlist for a racing yard out in the middle of nowhere with Ely shut.'

'I'm confident it'll survive, we'll be handing over a readymade business, owners and their horses are already here. And there are talents like Gunslinger and Pobble Beach among the ranks. If we don't do this, I'd be more worried about our marriage surviving.'

'Really? We're good Danny, aren't we?'

Danny nodded. 'But I've seen the toll this winter has taken on you. And it's sapped the life and soul from us. We're walking round like zombies half the time. Making the break now, perhaps Jack and Cerys would start seeing the best of us. You asked me would I give up all this, our life up here, and I said yes. Now you're the one getting cold feet.'

'What about Kegsy?'

'You can either switch him to a yard nearer London, or a trainer you'd trust …' Danny leant back and caught a glimpse of the staff photo on the wall. 'Wait! What about Jordi and Beth?'

'Would they take it on?'

'We can give them first refusal. They love it here, not just the horses, it's where they first met,' Danny said. 'They're part of this place, they make it run like clockwork and at least we'll know horses like Powder Keg are in safe hands. Jordi once even told me his dream was to become a trainer. We can make that happen. What do you say?'

She made a face. 'I can't believe this is happening.'

'You said we needed more time together and this will be our only chance before the kids settle into a school.'

'What did you tell the BHA?'

'I said I'd think about it.'

'Seriously, Danny, there's nothing much to think about.' Meg stood and leant over whispering something in his ear.

Danny sighed. 'I don't blame you.'

He picked up the phone and made the call.

197

'Sir Jacob Rice speaking.'
'When can I start?'

25457168R00113

Printed in Great Britain
by Amazon